Y0-DDQ-693

THE
MORRÍGAN'S
KEY

Kristin Schaeffer

To my daughter.
Finding my voice has changed my life in so
many ways.
May you find yours before you've ever lost it.

Especially for you –

Diane,
Best wishes!

ISBN: 978-1-63068-742-7

ACKNOWLEDGEMENTS

I want to take a moment to acknowledge all the great people who helped me, pushed me and helped make this book possible.

Thank you, Mama for reading it 3+ (?) times and doing the copy editing for me. I love you and I'm always grateful for your support. Thank you to Rachel Bouzis, who read and did an editor's job for me. You gave me some wonderful insights and weren't afraid to critique my writing. I needed that! I need to thank Diane Perry, Chelsea Smith, Jackie Perry, Brad Erickson, Lindsey Erickson, Nicole Crabb, and Teryn (my daughter), for being early readers and struggling through some of my first drafts. Your kindness and interest are much appreciated! Thank you, Walker. You put up with a lot of: "Could you please be quiet," and "Please settle down and let me write." I love you, little Buddy. Thank you Eric Lewis, for refusing the job to do the cover art. You pushed me to do it myself and I'm glad I did. This has been such a personal labor of love for me that I think my art on the cover is what it really needed. Eric, thank you also, for trying to read one of the very first drafts and getting invested in the story itself. Your encouragement meant a lot to me and really helped me keep going when I got discouraged. Thank you, Vicki Burger for reading and critiquing despite your aversion to YA. I love that you loved it! Thank you to my daddy for always believing in me. To hear you say you're proud of me lifts me up like none other. Thank you to my Pops and Grandmama for showing me that books can be the most lovely distraction when things get hairy. Your love of reading rubbed off and I'm so glad it did. Thank you also to my Grandma Perry who read a story I wrote at a very young age and bought me a magnet to put on my refrigerator that said: "I'm expecting a great idea any minute now!" I looked at it day in and day out for years and years growing up, and knew that you had faith I would do this someday. Thank you, Grandpa Perry for showing me what a great story teller is. I miss you and your funny stories so much.

Lastly, thank you to my husband, Jason. You're always a driving force in my life and you're the one who made this whole thing possible. Without your love and support, I'm not sure I would have ever gotten to a place mentally to be able to write this. Thanks for putting up with my nose in a computer, writing for hours on end and ignoring you on long trips so I could maximize the writing time as much as possible. Thank you mostly for loving me.

CHAPTER ONE

The Wall & the Gift

The meadow pulses with life all around me. I'm bathed in sunlight, lazily enjoying the buzzing symphony of bees humming their way across the field. I study the mountains in the distance, wondering what mysteries their jagged peaks might hold. I breathe in the freshness of the grasses and flowers, and watch a silent deer tip-toe through the farthest corner of the clearing.

My thoughts easily meander in the scene and it all creates a sense of peace and goodness that I've wondered if I would ever feel again. I think I just might stay here forever, sitting right here in this spot, free of responsibility in a place where right and wrong don't exist. Safe.

The quick movement of a faerie flitting from flower to flower in a dance with the bees catches my eye . . .

The record scratch of my thoughts grinding to a halt abruptly stops my mind's peaceful progression, pulling me back out of my reverie into this world around me.

A faerie?

On her way by, she stops to look at me, hovering only

inches from my face and my heartbeat picks up speed.

Unbelievable. I am eye to eye with a faerie!

Her eyes are bright and smiling and the colors of her hair and wings simply amazing! They shimmer purple, red, blue and gold. Swirling pigments bleed into each other like a watercolor painting.

Chirping like a little bird, she hovers close and picks up a tiny lock of my long, black hair and twirls it around her neck, wearing it like a scarf. She prances and poses playfully, making me laugh, which I try hard to do silently, afraid I might scare her away if I make any noise. I notice that something about her features is familiar. I feel like we are old friends.

Suddenly I become aware that the light is changing in the meadow and I look up to see clouds rolling in and the setting sun casting a red and orange hue over my surroundings, chasing away the peacefulness of the afternoon, making it feel eerie instead.

The buzzing of the bees grows louder and takes on a new pitch, and I look back to my faerie friend just in time to see her darting away with a smile and fleeting wave over her shoulder. The bees' buzzing grows in intensity and grates on my nerves while a white light blooms at the edge of the tree line and spreads, getting brighter until it becomes too bright to look at.

I open my eyes and make the inevitable transition from being asleep to awake. I'm in my bedroom and my happy mood immediately changes to grumpy.

Ugh! Stupid alarm!

As my groggy head starts to clear, bits and pieces of the dream start coming back. All at once my mind puts two and two together and I remember something spectacular: *The faerie!*

I jump out of bed and run to my desk where brushes, pencils, tubes of paint, paper, palettes and erasers are scattered everywhere.

I really gotta get this mess cleaned up . . . maybe I should go ahead and do that . . . no, wait. I was looking for something . . . what was it . . . ?

I dig through the piles of drawings and sketchbooks only vaguely aware of my original mission. When I get to one that I filled last month the fogginess clears a little more. I flip the pages, frantically looking.

I think I know . . .

I turn a page and come to a painting I had stashed between the pages of my sketchbook to help flatten out the paper.

There! I knew I had seen her before!

The faerie from my dream stares back at me. I not only know her, I painted her!

Lost in thought, I put the book and painting back down on my messy desk and pad down the stairs smiling, feeling cheerful again thinking about the dream faerie.

"Never dreamed about one of my paintings before . . . " I mumble under my breath as I walk into the kitchen.

Mama is already seated at our breakfast bar having her coffee.

"What was that, Dana?" she asks.

I just wave my hand at her shooing away her question like a pesky fly and shake my head irritably, feigning morning grog. I don't feel like sharing.

I sit down for breakfast and we commence our daily, absurd, one-way conversation.

Mama asks me things like: "What will you do at school today?" and "Did you finish all your homework?" and "Do you have art class today?"; while I give my one-word: "nothing", "yes" and "no" answers.

I know she asks because she wants to talk to me and can't think of anything else to talk about. It's her attempt to keep the lines of communication open even though I've closed them down.

Since the 'incident' last Spring it's too hard to talk to anyone, especially my parents. I feel different.

It's like there are two people inside me now warring against one another to take up the position of the prominent personality: this new, slightly bitter, negative me who sees the world through anger-tinted glasses, and the old me. The new me is cynical, more aware of her surroundings, less likely to throw her cares to the wind and laugh loudly. She feels sadness deeply, is easily hurt, and easily annoyed. I don't really like her much, but I'm sort of stuck with her at the moment.

The other side of me is who I was 'before'. She smiles a lot, loves art and beauty, and has a natural ability to find it in everything and everybody. She's positive, outgoing, upbeat and fun. Unfortunately, she's hiding. The events of that day have tainted her view of the world and she gives me over to the new, darker me most of the time. It makes me sad, but from time to time she stands her ground and tries to take control.

From somewhere outside myself I can see this fight happening, as if I am soaring above myself and watching a battle roar on. I am able to see both sides as clearly as if they were soldiers in a field shooting at each other. They don't like each other at all and the Dark Me is dead set on destroying the "Before Me".

Poor "Before Me". She mostly just defends herself while trying to lick her wounds and carry on. "Dark Me" thinks "Before Me" is weak and it's her fault that everything happened . . .

"Dana? You with me?"

"Oh, yeah, sorry Mama," I drag myself back into her interrogation.

When she's satisfied that I've answered enough questions, she stops talking and I pick up my cereal bowl, walk to the sink, rinse it out, and put it in the dishwasher. I find that if I at least do small, menial household chores, she leaves me alone and doesn't try to make me talk about my feelings so much.

I think she thinks as long as I can do normal stuff like dishes I must be feeling normal.

Little does she know I'm not.

I run back upstairs for the morning clean-up routine: shower, wash hair, dry hair, brush teeth, throw on any old jeans, t-shirt, hoodie and tennis shoes. I'm running late as usual, but it doesn't stop me from looking at my painted faerie one more time. I think about my dream again and what it's like to see my painting as a living thing.

My fingers trace the outline of her wings and I picture the way they shimmered. It makes me smile again, but I snap back to reality when Mama's voice pierces the bubble of my musing.

"Dana! You're late!"

I look at my clock, gasp, swooping up my backpack, run down the stairs two at a time, and out the door.

"Bye, Mama!" I yell and the door slams behind me.

Once outside my resolve to go to school wavers. So goes the old saying: the road to school is paved with good intentions.

Every morning I go through the motions of getting ready, and leaving (mostly) on time. I walk out my front door, down the front steps, and stop. I look in the direction I should go, but when I think about taking a step in that direction the memories of the ordeal come flooding back and I can't force myself to make the trip. I can't face anyone at school because, as ridiculous as it sounds, it feels like there's a sign on my head advertising that it happened. I feel like everyone knows and they all look at me with pity which, whether real or perceived, only serves to remind me that I'm now fundamentally different from my peers.

'The incident' and 'the ordeal' are names I've come up with so that I don't have to say the ugly phrase out loud. As if not saying it will make it go away and somehow make it less real. The therapist my mother finally took me to when she got over the initial denial that something terrible happened to me, thinks it's a bad idea. She wants me to come to terms with the words. She has me practice saying it in a sentence:

"I was date-raped and it was not my fault."

But deep down I can't believe that's true. What I hear in my head is:

"I was date-raped and it was all my fault. If I hadn't been drinking tequila straight from the bottle I would have been able to push that asshole off of me when I said no."

I turn my face upward and soak in the sun rays that seem to warm me from the inside out. Even though it's late October, the temperature is balmy. It helps pick up my spirits immediately, even so, just like most days, instead of turning left to go to school, I turn right to walk to my favorite place to be with my new best friends named paper, pencil and music.

And off I go!

Not far from my house is a state park where I love to hike because there are never any people there. I can be deliciously alone all day without ever seeing a soul. It's really the perfect place for a truant high-schooler determined to avoid everyone she knows indefinitely.

On my way, I walk silently down the sidewalk, past all the stately, Antebellum homes in our town with their sturdy foundations and neoclassical facades. I entertain myself by giving some thought to brief stories for each family that lives in them. I imagine what they look like, what kind of jobs they have, how many children live there, and what they're like.

About the time I exhaust my imagination, the houses nestled on their city blocks give way to long, winding roads with farm houses spread much farther apart, and all I have to look at are the trees.

I notice the golden colors of their leaves and the sound of the breeze rustling through them. Fall is nearing it's end and some of the leaves are beginning to turn brown. Their tap, tap, tapping makes me think they might crumble and fall apart at any second, kind of like me.

I wish I could just stay outside all the time. Out here life is just easier.

When I'm in the open, under the sky, I can feel my thoughts flow like a river unobstructed. The air and sun chase away the dark thoughts that otherwise dam up my mind. It's really the only time I feel like myself anymore and it feels too good to ruin it all by going to school.

Finally, I arrive at my destination.

Ah, my day begins.

About 500 yards past the main entrance of the park, but before a bridge, a trail juts off to the road to the right and follows the river, bypassing the main gate. Sneaking in makes me feel bad, but I don't have any money, and lately feeling compelled to do the right thing doesn't last very long.

Without another thought I step onto the trail and duck into the trees. Immediately I am an animal of the forest: sure-footed and lithe without a worry in the world and I know that under the trees I can do anything I put my mind to. I get a taste of what it would be like to feel special again.

Sometimes it seems like the forest birds are calling out just for me to tell me that everything is going to be alright. The tug of their songs urges me to listen. The twinkling notes swirl around me as if on wings themselves, mingling with the wind in the trees, the rush of the river, the chirp of the crickets, and the swelling hiss of the cicadas, forming a musical masterpiece that makes me wonder if other people hear the same things I do, because it seems like if they did, someone would record it and make millions.

Maybe it's because this is no ordinary forest and other people haven't discovered it yet. In addition to its impromptu concerts it holds mysteries untold. I've been here dozens of times and curiously each time I'm here there's something new to see.

Today's surprise is a short, moss-covered, stone wall; an extension of a small hill next to the trail. I can understand how I've previously passed it by, as it appears to be weathered, and could easily be mistaken for a natural pile of stone. A part of me wonders if gnomes didn't magically build it here this morning, just for me.

What was it built for? Is this someone's ancient home? What's the story of this place? Who built it? Did a family live here? What

8

were they like? I wish there was some way to find out.

I look it over carefully for clues and I can see places where the edges of the block aren't smooth because time has worn it down, chipping off great chunks and rounding the edges in others. When I stand back and look at the main body of the wall from a distance, the definite man-made lines of cut stone are evident. I am fascinated by the hidden story of this place. A good mystery always piques my interest.

Hmm, let's explore!

Starting where the wall comes out of its hill I run my hands along its surface. It is cool and damp, smooth, rough, solid, and soft all at the same time. The lush green of the moss growing on the blocks nearly blots out the grey of the stone, making it a living being with a stone skeleton and mossy skin. Standing only seven or eight feet high, and spanning only around twelve feet in length, one probably wouldn't classify it as a large wall. The blocks are about a foot thick, and it seems old, maybe even ancient, but it's still solid. Time hasn't compromised its integrity.

I feel privileged as I inspect it. *What if I am the only modern person who has ever seen it; like an archeologist who digs at something spectacular that's been out in plain view, because he just happens to be the person that recognized it was something special?*

I continue to the end and find that thick bushes and vines have wrapped themselves around it to form another wall of greenery back to the hillside. I want to see the other side of the wall, so I push through the mass of bushes at a thin spot.

Inside it's spacious - like a room cut off from the world except that the top is completely open so it's flooded with light. I stand and admire my discovery.

My very own, private, outdoor room. What a perfect place to spend my day!

I sling my maroon backpack, covered in painted symbols of my own design, off my back, walk deeper into my new hideout and excitedly flop down onto the leaf-carpeted floor. I drag my pack onto my lap and pull out my newest sketch book and some pencils to draw with. I prop the pack against the wall and lean on it, getting comfortable.

The mysterious, moss-covered wall gets me thinking of the equally mysterious faerie of my dream, so I decide to draw her again in a different pose, and set to work, enjoying being outside and listening to the music of the forest. Bird song, bright sunlight, fresh air and the scratch of a pencil moving across paper relaxes me and gets the creative juices flowing.

I get lost in my drawing, taking great care with the details of her hair and wings, until the sun is high over head. I'm shading, working out some details, when a movement catches my eye pulling me out of my work. Two little birds are perched on the top of the wall - the source of the song I've been listening to while I sketched.

Must be curious that I found this place. Guess they they don't see people here much.

I look back down to my paper, drawing only a few moments longer before another movement, this time at my feet, catches my eye again.

One of the little birds has flown down and is singing his pretty song right in front of me! When he finishes, his friend on the wall echoes the exact same song. It would seem they are singing to each other, but . . . they're looking at me.

How odd . . . but so cute!

They do this a few more times, then fly away, but the song has weaseled its way into my head as any catchy tune is likely to do. I hear myself humming their song to myself as I draw. At first I only barely remember it. I hum it softly and miss a few notes, but after a couple of tries I get it right and hum a little louder, more confidently.

I'm just finishing up the drawing, humming and putting on the finishing touches when my black and white pencil drawing of the faerie from my dream suddenly bursts into color from head to toe! Some of the lines of the drawing begin to move and pop off the page while some of them seem stuck to it.

I gasp and slam the sketch book shut!

I must have fallen asleep . . . right? I'm dreaming?

My heart is pounding, but everything around me looks normal: the light, the wall, the leaves on the ground, my backpack. I feel awake.

I open the sketchbook just a crack to the page where I had been drawing and my faerie is still there, in black and white exactly the way I drew her.

Whew! I must be losing my mind! Maybe I'm just tired . . .

I put my head back against the wall and close my eyes and immediately drift off.

CHAPTER TWO

The Meeting

When I realize I'm dreaming again it's because I find myself back in the same meadow from the dream I had last night, but this time I'm leaning on my backpack, with my head against the wall from the park. It's as if someone picked me up along with everything I was touching and put me down in the meadow.

I continue to sit there - a little unsure of what is happening to me.

Am I really asleep or is this some crazy thing my brain is manufacturing? Am I losing my mind?

I raise my hand up to look at it, turning it over, looking first at the palm of my hand, then at the back. I pinch my other arm and it sure feels real! I seem to be in control of my body which is very different from every other dream I've ever had in my life.

I sit forward slowly and look around. Everything is exactly the same as in my dream from last night. Even the deer is in position at the edge of the clearing.

Directly in front of me a leaf on a flower stem moves and a tiny pair of aqua blue eyes peer over it at me. I crane my neck to get a better look.

It's my faerie!

When I smile she zooms out into the open and again flies right up to my face, beaming at me excitedly. My smile doesn't falter, even though I'm really confused about what's happening. It's pretty amazing to see something I painted as a living thing even if it is in a dream.

She's chirping at me again. *Is she trying to talk to me?*

"I don't understand," I say shaking my head and shrugging my shoulders.

An idea blooms on her face like a lightbulb being switched on.

She flies up and kisses my cheek, and an energy more gentle than electricity, but similarly intense courses through my body.

It isn't unpleasant, but I shiver at the unique experience.

The faerie looks at me expectantly, then tries out her voice again. It sounds like the bird song at first, but changes gradually, becoming choppy, then smoothing out until she is speaking English.

" . . . thought you would never get me off that page. There is so much I need to tell you!"

I'm definitely dreaming, I laugh to myself. *Most lifelike dream I've ever had, despite it's weirdness.*

She looks annoyed at my flippant laugh. "This is serious."

"Oh. Well okay, I'm sorry. It's just that I know I'm dreaming."

She flashes me a dramatic scowl, flies to stand on my hand, and . . . pinches me? She's so tiny that it feels like a bug bite or bee sting, a little painful, and shocking.

13

I suck in my breath, let out an alarmed squeak, and scramble up and over my backpack, trying to get away from her, but there's nowhere to go. My back is against the wall from the park.

I scowl back for an instant, then realize I'm not dreaming!

"Wha . . .? I don't . . . I'm going crazy! What is happening to me?!"

She looks at me for a long moment. Silence hangs between us like a curtain then she slowly flies closer and closer until she is only a couple of inches from my face. Apprehension forces me to recoil.

"I'm sorry I pinched you," she says gently. "May I?"

I don't know what she is asking to do, but I nod.

She carefully approaches my face and nestles against my cheek in what I can only describe as a tiny hug for lack of a better term. Calm descends over me like a warm blanket, and I know everything is okay.

Wow . . . that was . . . strange.

"Is that better?" she asks.

I close my eyes and marvel at how her 'hug' feels very much like the sun on my face on this morning's walk.

"Yes," I say. "You scared me a little at first. Well . . . not you, just that you're . . . you know, here."

"It's okay," she says hovering at eye level. "I understand it isn't every day in the human world that a painting comes to life."

"So you really are my painting?!" I ask her excitedly, forgetting for a moment that I must be losing my marbles.

She smiles broadly, nodding.

"Yes, I am! Or at least I was!"

"But I don't understand," I say. "What is going on?"

"Well, first things first," she giggles. "Introductions are in order! My name is Aurelia. I have been waiting two thousand years to be reborn just to give you a message I've been guarding for you all that time! Merlin made me promise not to ever speak it aloud until I could give it to you."

"You have a message for me? From Merlin? Like . . . Merlin the magician?!"

Her head bobs up and down and she grins from ear to ear. She lands on my knee and marches back and forth with her hands on her hips and her chest puffed out as she explains.

I stifle a little laugh.

"Yes! Merlin only trusted me enough to carry your message. Because I am a brave faerie I was given the task!" she says proudly.

"I can certainly see that you are," I say, smiling and nodding, and I try to steer her back to the subject at hand.

"But what was the message you brought from Merlin?"

"Oh! Yes, yes. I'm sorry. I got a bit off track, didn't I?" She straightens herself up hands at her side and clears her throat.

"Ahem!

It is only when notes and ink intermingle
that the Bard the barrier doth break,
in the Otherworld is where the Bard doth wake.
Here what once was flat, now within doth Awen dwell,
all destined a piece of Brighid's Prophecy to foretell."

I look at her blankly. I have no idea what she has just said. "What does it mean?"

"Well," she starts, "It means that you can bring anything you draw or paint to life here in the Otherworld! And there are things you must draw to learn about the Prophecy."

My mind is racing and I fire question after question at her.

"I can . . . do what? Bring my art to life? What is the Otherworld?"

"Yes! Today you started the magic in the human world, but you went to sleep before it was finished. You woke up here where the magic takes place. You can only give us life here. As for where this is or what it is . . . you'll have to discover that for yourself. Sometime very soon you'll get to ask questions of people who have answers for you."

Aurelia's hands fly about wildly while she talks. Her eyes grow wide, then she narrows them and jumps up and down to emphasize her points. It's quite comical to watch and makes me forget to listen to what she is actually saying.

I suddenly remember that I am supposedly in this Otherworld place.

"So the Otherworld is what . . . some parallel universe or something?"

"No, not exactly, but as I said, I am not the one to explain it all. My purpose was to deliver the messages to start with, and now to be your companion on the journey," she says. "Merlin will be sending more messages, you just have to find them."

With that she smiles hugely and flops down on my knee as if to say that was all she's going to say on the matter.

"Find them? How am I going to do that?" Aurelia

closes her eyes and shakes her head tipping her head back slightly in a smug gesture of secrecy.

"Well do you know how I get home at least?" I ask.

"Oh yes! That is important isn't it? All you have to do is draw the place you wish to be and sing while you draw. That should do it."

I look around at the meadow feeling unsure. I have no idea if I'm dreaming, if I've gone insane, or I really am in some other place.

All I have to do is draw where I want to be? This is completely nuts . . .

I pick up my sketchbook which is already open to a blank page and start to draw a forest with a stone wall while I sing the pretty song the birds were singing earlier. I put the final touches on the drawing and close my eyes just for a minute when I start to feel tired and when I open them I gasp. I am in the park again sitting the way I was in my 'dream' with the sketchbook in my hands, but the page is blank!

Where did it go?!

I flip through the pages and the drawing of the park and the wall is gone. But then so is my drawing of the faerie I did earlier . . . *This is just too weird . . .*

It's starting to get dark and the forest is quiet as if the birds have gone to bed. I stand up reaching for my backpack, but it's gone too.

Oh no! I must have left it in the Otherworld! All my school books! My computer! How in the world am I going to be able to explain this? And I'm going to be late for dinner!

Running all the way home I don't have much time to think. I can only concentrate on not dying since I am not much of a runner.

When I get to my house I leap onto the front porch

and as quietly as I can, open the front door only as far as I have to in order to slide through it. Once I'm about half way up the stairs I yell out my greeting hoping to make it up to my room before my mom sees that I'm only carrying a sketchbook and a pencil.

"Hey Mama!"

Once inside my room I flop down on my bed, huffing and puffing, trying to catch my breath, and while I rest, the day's events replay in my head like a movie. I'm not even sure what to think of it all.

When I can finally breathe without gasping for breath, I decide it's safe to go downstairs. I push up from the bed and notice a piece of water color paper on the floor leaning against my desk.

What . . . ?

As I walk over I notice that my faerie painting isn't on top of my desk where I left it. "I must have dropped it on my way out the door this morning." I say out loud to myself, but when I pick it up and turn it over my heart skips a beat.

It's blank.

Baffled, I stand there a minute trying to figure out what this all means. I can't be hallucinating. I've read before that when people hallucinate they can't wonder if they're crazy because they are. The clinically insane just think it's real without questioning. I'm fairly sure I'm not dreaming because my backpack really disappeared. I know I didn't leave it anywhere. I had been laying on it!

That only leaves one possibility: it must all be real.

So what now?

Aurelia mentioned a prophecy, some place I actually went today called the Otherworld, more messages from Merlin coming soon.

This is not happening!

I'm feeling overwhelmed. I glance at my alarm clock and it's 6 o'clock!

I'd better get downstairs for dinner before Mom comes up here and thinks I'm acting weird.

Downstairs in the kitchen I smile at her, trying to appear as normal as possible. "Hi Mama." I manage a perfectly normal tone, despite my churning thoughts of craziness.

I should think about maybe being an actress when I grow up, I'm pretty good at it.

"Hi D," she says returning my smile and coming to hug me. "Come help me get dinner on the table, please?"

"Sure, Mom."

She hands me two plates, two forks, two knives and two napkins, then picks up the hot dog casserole she's made and follows me into the dining room.

"Dad's away tonight?" I ask, a little grateful that I don't have to act for two parents.

"Yeah," she sighs, "He had a dinner meeting to go to in Savannah."

My parents are very close, but my dad is a contractor for a company that does training seminars for managers of big box stores all over the Southeast. It takes him away from home a lot and I know that Mama misses him. A couple of years ago she started doing his books and billing so she could quit her job and just work for him. This helped them spend a little more time together, but they still have to be apart often.

I set the table for us, we sit down to eat, and Mama starts with the questions.

"How was your day?"

Oh here we go, absurd-conversation-of-the-day number two.

19

It's a normal question to anyone other than me, but in my house it means that, once again, she doesn't know what else to say.

"Fine, Mama. Nothing to report, really. Same old, same old. School, you know?"

Ha! Today was nothing short of the weirdest day I've ever had in my life, but if I tell you how it really went, you'll put me in a mental institution before I can blink.

"Well, you didn't do anything interesting today?"

"No, Mama."

"Are you sure? Nothing unusual happened?"

Or maybe she knows exactly what to say? Does she know something?!

"No, nothing happened, Mama. Is there something I should know?" I ask her, feeling like I'm busted.

"Well the school called."

Oh great. I am.

"They said you haven't been to class at all this week, and evidently your attendance has been pretty spotty since the beginning of the year.

"Oh . . . well, yeah. There's that, I guess."

"Dana, what's going on? You're failing out of your senior year! Your principal said, the way things are now, if you can't get a handle on your school-work pretty quickly, you'll be repeating it."

Now at this point, I have to give my mom some credit. She doesn't seem to get mad when things like this come up, just "concerned".

I prop my head on my fist, elbow on the table - a total no-no in any good southern home.

"Dana!" My mother instantly corrects me.

"Right! Sorry!" I say, and jerk my elbow away like the table is made of hot coals, then mindlessly push the casserole around on my plate with my fork wondering what in the world to tell her. The truth? Another lie? Neither one seems like a good option.

What about a version of the truth?

After a long silence with Mama's stare burning a hole through me, I finally think of something somewhat acceptable to say.

"Mama, the truth is I just don't know how to go to school now. I mean . . . being around all those people is just too much. Sometimes I feel like I'm suffocating. I turn a corner and he's there or his friends are. Every time I see them flashes of that night come to me. I can see everything happening and it feels like I'm back there going through it all again. I just don't want to go. I can't relive the ordeal every day like that."

A tear wells up and threatens to spill out of my right eye. I sniffle and blink it back.

"Dana . . ." She tries to hide the pity in her face, but she isn't as good at acting as I am. "What do you want to do? You can't just quit school."

"I know. I wish I could," I say admittedly. "What about homeschool? I only have a little over a semester left. I could finish it up on an online program or something . . . "

"Do you think you can manage that?" she asks. "You'll be basically teaching yourself."

"I don't know, Mama. I guess I won't really know until I try it, but it has to be better than dreading school so much that I can't even force myself to go."

"That's true. Let me talk to your dad about it and we'll probably give Dr. Flannigan a call and talk it over with her, too. You can stay home this week, but expect to either start homeschool or go back to school next week, ok?"

"Ok, Mama, that's fair."

Huh! Go figure. It turned out to be more than another absurd conversation after all. My mom really listened to me. Have I entered the twilight zone, or what?

We finish up the rest of dinner in silence. When it's over, I clear the table and put the dishes in the dishwasher, pushing the theory that normalcy is still the best cover.

Maybe it will convince Mama that I can handle homeschooling myself.

I walk out to the living room where my mom is reading in her favorite chair.

"I'm going to head to bed early tonight, Mama. I'm kind of tired."

"Ok," she says motioning me over for a good night hug.

"Love you."

"Love you too, D."

I head upstairs and dress for bed, peel back my sheets and climb in. I lay there staring up at my ceiling for a long time just letting the random thoughts run through my head. Today was one of the most eventful days I've had in a long time. Some things got close to being resolved, while others got even more complicated.

Just when my eyelids get droopy and I feel like closing them, a purple light comes zooming up to my bed and lands on my extra pillow. It's my faerie!

"Aurelia! What are you doing here?"

"Just because your art comes to life in the Otherworld, doesn't necessarily mean your creations stay there. By the way, you forgot something today when you left." She smiles and gestures toward the desk where my backpack hangs on the back of my chair.

"Oh my gosh! You brought it back for me? How did you do that?"

She chuckles and curls her arms up to make muscles. "I may be small, but I am mighty!" I laugh and she doubles over giggling hysterically, rolling around on the pillow.

Wow, she's really here!

"May I?" I ask her reaching out toward her wings.

"Of course, just be careful. They're fragile like the wings of a butterfly."

I softly touch just the edge and it feels like rice paper. Next I touch her hair and it reminds me of goose down - so soft. *I can't believe I'm touching a faerie!*

"I spoke with Merlin today after you left the Otherworld, Dana. I was supposed to let him know when my message had been delivered, so I went to find him. He sent another one for you."

"He did? I don't understand why I can't just go see him myself?"

"All in due time, Dana. You will see him when you are ready, but it isn't time for that yet."

I'm a little disappointed. "Okay."

"But he asked me to tell you that he needs you to go back to the wall tomorrow. It warrants a closer inspection. It's a special place, but you knew that already, didn't you?"

"Yes, I suppose I did. I kind of felt it."

"I thought you might have. Merlin says you're a special Bard."

"What is a Bard anyway? The first message from Merlin mentions that word."

She wags her finger at me smiling broadly.

"Uh, uh, uh, Dana. I told you. I am only the messenger, your guide. Besides, I don't know what the answers are," her exaggerated shrug makes her look mischievous.

CHAPTER THREE

Séamus & the Plan

I wake up to my alarm and slap it off. There's no reason I need to get up at any particular time today. I roll over to go back to sleep and realize I didn't dream at all.

A normal night's sleep. Maybe this means a normal day? Was it all just a dream?

My thoughts churning, I sit up to get my day started. There won't be any more sleep for me this morning. As I slide out of bed I see a spot of purple on my other pillow.

Not a dream.

Aurelia is still right where she fell asleep talking to me.

I've had one whole day to get used to the idea of magic drawings and being a Bard, (whatever that is), and it's really not any easier to accept today than it was yesterday. I wonder how long it's going to take for my new reality to feel real?

Man, it does feel good not to have to worry about school though.

The only thing I need to do today is figure out what it is that a legendary, ancient magician wants me to find out about the wall in the park.

Going to school might be easier.

I run downstairs to gulp down a bowl of oatmeal, hurry through morning clean-up, and when I emerge from the bathroom, Aurelia is preening in front of my mirror.

I laugh out loud and she jumps like I've scared her.

"I thought you had painted another faerie! Then when she moved exactly the same way I did I realized it was only water. But why is it hard? It can't be frozen . . . it isn't cold."

When I laugh even harder her eyebrows knit together and a scowl appears on her face.

"It isn't nice to laugh at people." she barks, stomping a foot.

I force my face into one of false remorse, (which isn't easy) and run to her trying not to laugh the whole time. Reaching down, I scoop her up and bring her to my face, close my eyes and present my cheek.

"Hug me," I say. "It isn't the same as me hugging you, but I can't really do it."

She laughs and gives me a 'hug' and I turn her around to face the mirror again. I tap it with my fingernail so she can hear how it sounds, then walk to the window and tap that with my nail as well.

"See," I tell her. "It's only glass. It's just that the mirror has a coating on the back that reflects and doesn't let you see through it."

Her eyes light up like a curious child and she gets very excited. She flies to the mirror and knocks on it with her tiny fist, barely making a noise, then flies to the window to do the same. She looks back at me grinning and nodding.

"Oh, I see now!" she says and we laugh together. It feels really good.

"I haven't laughed like this since before the Spring . . ." I tell her, my smile fading a bit when I remember. I wish so hard at that moment that I could just forget, but the time between remembering does seem to be getting longer, so that's something at least.

"How did you lose your laugh?" she asks me innocently.

I just look at her and the world around me stands completely still. It's moments like these when I feel just how big the chasm of separation is between me and everything else.

How to explain that to something so pure and untouched by sadness? Impossible.

"I'm not sure how to explain it to you. Maybe one day I will be able to, but not now," I say and I wave my hand in front of my face like I can brush it away as easy as that. "Let's get going on our mission today! I have an idea for how I can take you with me without being seen."

I grab my backpack and hoist it onto the bed. I pull out the books and notebooks that I would need if I were going to school and put in a blanket and a lunch I packed while I was downstairs for breakfast. My stomach was pretty rumbly when I came home from the park yesterday.

"Come look," I wave Aurelia over. "There's a little mesh pocket on the side of my backpack. Someone could see you, but only if they looked very closely. This way, at least, you won't be flying along beside me freaking people out."

"Okay . . . " she says. "I could just be there already. No one would see me, but I think I would rather stay with you."

She shoots up off the bed and drops silently into the

pocket.

"We're ready to go!"

Relieved that I can spend my day the way I want to without the stress of feeling like I need to be at school, and excited for my day of adventure, I scoop up the backpack and sling it onto my back. I rush downstairs, and out the door.

"Bye, Mama!"

I take the trip to the park at a near run, or at least a speed walk. This day is just too exciting for a stroll. The new world opening up to me has taken over my thoughts and I can't think of anything else.

I arrive at the trail and realize I didn't see anything on the way, didn't imagine a single story about a house, didn't notice anything about the trees. I chuckle at my one-track mind and duck into the forest on the trail. It's sunny again today and the trail is ablaze with light. When I get there, the wall seems to be glowing and a crow sits atop it today, a silent observer.

Just a trick of the sunlight.

I walk to the end, just like yesterday and duck inside my 'outdoor room'.

When I was here before I got distracted by how amazingly secret it felt and forgot why I had entered the 'room' in the first place. I had wanted to inspect the other side of the wall since it is completely hidden from view.

Inside my secret room I put my backpack down gently, pull open the pocket, and Aurelia flies out and stretches. She arches her back, extending her arms high above her head, pointing her toes, and curls her hands into fists. She flies a couple of loop-da-loops and I look on with amazed laughter.

"That pocket is pretty cramped," she says pouting, but

her face changes immediately when she spots the wall. "Oh! There it is! Let's get started!"

I look at her incredulously. "What are we supposed to get started doing exactly?"

"Well I don't really know," she shrugs, "Merlin just said you should take a closer look at the wall, that's all. So let's look!"

Aurelia flies to the wall and hovers along each row, inspecting every block, so I join in. I run my hands over the blocks one by one starting with the top left and moving to the right.

What am I looking for?

I'm about two rows from the top and three blocks from the right when Aurelia zooms up to me. Her eyes are huge!

"I found something!" She squeals, and darts back to the block she had been examining, with me trailing behind, failing miserably at keeping up.

Wow, that faerie is fast!

She points to a block that is sticking out of the side of the hill about four rows down from the top. When I look closely I can just make out an irregularity peeking out from under the moss on its surface. I gently peel the green moss back and there are five beautiful symbols carved in the stone. They're wonderfully artistic and decorative, but unlike anything I have ever seen. Some of them are made of hard lines and angles and some are entirely made of swirl patterns. The grooves of the carving have smoothed out, obviously not freshly done, so I know they're definitely old.

Amazing! Who could have carved these?

I pull a sketchbook out to draw them, and prop my feet on my backpack.

They must mean something, but what? And how can I find out?

Aurelia perches on my shoulder to watch me work and as I get the drawing close to being finished she flies down to the page and looks up at me.

"Dana, sing while you draw . . ."

"Oh! Right. I completely forgot. I suppose if I am supposed to learn something from these things that may help, huh?"

So I return to my drawing and Aurelia returns to my shoulder. I hum the bird songs that I sang while working on my drawing of her yesterday, and a second later the lines start to pop off the page in places and I know that's my cue to close my eyes.

When I open them, the wall, Aurelia and I are in the meadow in the Otherworld and something is happening on the block. The lines of the symbols are all beginning to move, unfurling and rearranging themselves into a rectangle. As they settle, they separate from the surrounding block and appear to form a smaller block inset in the original one.

"Aurelia! What do you think it is?"

"I don't know, but it looks like you could pry it out. I think you should try it!"

I push tentatively on one corner and the small block moves slightly. Encouraged I wedge my fingers into the grooves on each end of the rectangle and pull. There's almost nothing to grip and it takes a few tries, but I finally get it moving. Aurelia flies up to the hole it left in the bigger block and lights herself up.

"Wow! You're better than a flashlight!" I say smiling at her.

"What's a flashlight?" she asks.

"Remind me to show you when we get home," I say

absentmindedly as I peer into the hole, distracted by something inside. "What is that?" I say mostly to myself.

I reach in and grasp something cold and hard and pull it out. When I open my hand I'm holding what looks like some kind of ancient key. The top is carved with some of the same symbols that were carved into the stone and the shaft of the key has four sides, but it has been twisted several times decoratively. The end has notches cut out on all four edges and a small triangle that protrudes from one of the flat sides. I look at Aurelia.

"What a beautiful key! What do you think it goes to and what do you suppose I'm to do with it?"

She looks at me and shakes her head. "I am only the messenger, Dana . . ."

"I know, I know. You don't have any of the answers," I say rolling my eyes and heaving a great sigh.

I turn my attention back to the key studying it, turning it over, tracing all it's lines with my fingers.

I wish I knew what this is for!

Exasperated I stow the key in my jeans pocket and look beyond the wall to the meadow that I've been in a few times now, but never explored.

"Let's look around!" I say. "There's no place we need to be right now and Mama won't be expecting me home for hours yet."

"Okay!" Aurelia says.

I gather up my sketchbook with blank pages where my drawings keep disappearing, my pencil, and tuck both away inside the backpack.

At this rate I'll never need to buy another sketchbook.

"Let's go." I say returning my backpack to my back.

She flies out ahead of me and I start walking. There's nothing but forest on all sides of the clearing. The mountains look inviting and they've been beckoning since the first time I saw them in my dream, but I think it would take much longer to get to them than we have today.

That doesn't mean I can't have a look around at things closer.

"Aurelia, if I made you, where do these other faeries come from? Can they talk like you?"

"There are all manner of creatures here in the Otherworld. Things you've read about in books and things you've never even imagined. Some of them good and others very bad. These faeries were here before me and they can talk, but I don't think you would be able to understand them because they don't have a connection to you the way I do. I can give you the gift of understanding because you're my creator. But even when you hear me speaking to you now, I am not really speaking your language, you just hear your language. Any other human overhearing this would hear the same thing you did before I gave you the kiss."

"Ah," I say smiling. *Finally, an answer to a question.*

I turn my attention back to our surroundings.

The Meadow is so beautiful. As we walk through it I'm struck by how many different kinds of wild flowers there are in so many different colors. We reach the edge of the forest and I look at Aurelia again questioningly.

"Should we venture in a little?"

She nods at me excitedly and I can tell she is craving a bit of adventure just as much as I am. "Yes, I think it would be okay."

We tentatively enter the forest and I notice right away how different it is from the forests I'm used to. The trees have long, bare trunks all the way to the top where branches appear to have awkwardly exploded out of the end. The canopy it forms high over head gives the feeling of containment like an enclosure. There is a little light that is able to slip in and it reflects off everything around us creating a soft glow. Adding to the open feeling under the canopy is the lack of ground cover. There are only a few scrubby little bushes scattered around and piles of moss covered boulders

All around me this world feels fresh and clean and the air smells of pine and damp earth. I close my eyes and inhale deeply, loving the fresh air. It's a bit cooler here than it was in the meadow and significantly cooler than it was at home and a great shiver passes through me. Aurelia must have noticed. She flies up to nuzzle against my face and her sunshine warmth courses through me again, making me instantly more comfortable. I smile at her gratefully.

We go a bit further and just ahead under the canopy we see a tiny cottage with lights gleaming in the windows and smoke billowing from the rock chimney. I get a feeling that this is a good place and I know that we will be welcome here.

"I think we should knock. I'm not dressed for these temperatures. We could stop and warm up by the fire and eat our lunch."

Aurelia smiles. "Very well."

As we near the door, I can hear movement inside and despite my initial good feeling, fear of the unknown creeps into my thoughts.

I hope I'm right and whoever is inside is friendly.

I reach out to knock and hesitate, looking at Aurelia. She nods encouragingly and smiles, urging me on.

I knock lightly on the heavy wooden door, and hold my breath as I wait. Seconds later the door opens slowly, just wide enough for a large, brown eye to peer out. The eye scans me and then Aurelia and falls back on me before I hear a little gasp.

The door opens and we can see a small round man with a balding head sporting a ring of curly grey hair around the sides and back. He is wearing a pair of reading glasses low on his nose. His face is kind, with round cheeks and a wide smile from ear to ear. He holds his hands out wide in a gesture of welcome.

"Come in! Come in!" he exclaims loudly in something similar, but not identical to, an Irish accent. "I had begun ta think you were never goin' ta get here!"

I look at him in a state of shock. For the second time in two days my mouth won't form any words.

He knows me? Knew I was coming?

"Sit here by the fire, young one. You look half frozen!" he says motioning to a huge, furry rug in front of the hearth.

I sit down on the luxurious fur and continue to look at him in disbelief.

Things just get more and more bizarre.

There are a few moments of awkward silence and the little man begins to behave awkwardly. He wrings his hands glancing from me to Aurelia like he isn't sure what to say next.

Aurelia looks at him expectantly.

"Oh, I'm sorry," he says. "Where are my manners? The name's Séamus. Who might you be?" He hints that my manners are lacking which immediately forces me to take stock of them, putting me back into my typical southern gentile state of mind.

My mother would be horrified!

"I'm Dana and this is Aurelia," I say, but I'm confused.

". . . I thought you knew who we were . . . ?"

"Oh yes, I do," he begins, "but I didn't know yer name, only that you were comin'."

"I beg your pardon for asking," I say, "but how could you now that?"

"Merlin told me, of course!" he smiles broadly, obviously proud of his association.

"You know Merlin too?" I ask excitedly.

"Aye, young one, I do. And I have a message for you from him: He says you need ta stay in the Otherworld for a while. You've got ta start trainin'; the sooner the better!"

I blink at him, completely stunned.

Merlin, this person I've only ever heard of in stories, who seems to know everything about me, whom I've never met, wants me to do what?

"Séamus, I'm a student in the Human World and I still live with my parents. I can't just drop everything and come to live in the Otherworld. Besides, where would I stay? How would I support myself?"

"Oh now, you can stay right here, of course!"

"Well that's very generous of you, but I just don't know, Séamus. I want answers to my millions of questions more than anything, but I just don't see how I can do it. I have to finish school. I'm already behind and I only have a couple of months left. I can't just quit now. And please don't take this the wrong way, but I've only just met you and you want me to come live in your house for a while? That's just not something I would normally do." I say skeptically.

He looks disappointed, but resolute. "Yer just going ta have ta figure it out. It's going ta be necessary for you ta be here. There are things you need ta be taught and practice before you can move on."

Well, we aren't exactly getting off on the right foot are we? I look down, trying not to show the conflict I'm feeling.

I decide to just try to move forward with this moment and figure out the rest later.

"Ok well, I have a few questions that I wonder if you can help me with today."

"I'll try my best." he says smiling.

"The first time I left the Otherworld to go home, Aurelia told me I could go somewhere just by drawing the place and singing while I draw. Is that true only for the Otherworld? Or can I do it in the human world too?"

"Aye, you can do it anywhere. In the human world it's just going ta take a stronger song."

"So the songs are what works the magic? And there are different ones?"

Séamus nods smiling. "Aye."

"Can you teach me?"

Again Séamus nods. "Aye."

He immediately launches into a song and I can feel the notes flow through me. It's like my body recognizes them, as if I already know them somewhere deep inside myself.

I join in when he starts each song a second time around, and we sing together for hours. He shows me the songs first, tells me what they're for, then has me repeat them. He critiques my efforts, correcting me when I hit a wrong note, directing me to sing the songs over and over.

When darkness falls outside in the forest, I realize that I'm going to be walking home in the dark from the park now.

I had better figure out how to get home a better way.

"When you start ta learn the Bard songs with words you'll be able ta really do some magic then!" he says jubilantly, evidently pleased by our progress today.

"That will be a lot of fun!" I say. "But right now I need to start home. I've been thinking about it this afternoon and I promise I will see what I can do about coming to stay with you for a while."

"Alright then! I hope I'll see you again soon!" He smiles and hugs me and I know I've made another new friend.

I pull out my sketch book, put my backpack on my back, and I start to draw the wall in the park. It's the only place I can pop into where I know I won't be seen. Aurelia slips into her pocket just as I begin a perfect rendition of a new song that Séamus just taught me, and I see him smile just before I close my eyes.

When I open them, I am in the park at my wall again. It's almost completely dark, so walking the trail to get out of the park is a tough task. When I get out onto the street and the walking is easy, I go through the trip on auto-pilot while I think about how to work out a way to go live in the Otherworld.

I finally make it home to find Mama in the living room.

"Hi, Dana. How was your day?" she asks smiling at me.

"It was nice, Mama," I answer.

"What did you do? I meant to ask what you've been doing this whole time instead of going to school," she says.

"Oh! I go to the park," I say excitedly. "I love it there. I mostly just hang out with the birds."

And my faerie, and my friend Séamus . . .

"Well that sounds nice, but a little lonely." She looks at me with a sideways glance.

"It's not. There's no other way I want to spend my day," I tell her, but she scrutinizes me.

Looking for some sign of crazy, I'm sure.

"Okay. If you're sure," then after a short pause. "Dad will be home for dinner tonight. I thought we could all talk about a plan for school for you then."

"Okay, Mama, that works. I'm going to go upstairs and put on PJs and work on some art before dinner. Call me when dinner is ready?"

"Sure," she says.

I head upstairs and close my door. I pull out my computer, swipe some art supplies to the side on my desk, and set it up. I started working out a plan on the walk home, but I need to do some online research to help cement the pieces. While I wait for the computer to boot up I change into my pajamas and talk to Aurelia.

"What are you going to do?" She asks.

"Well I have about half a plan worked out in my head," I tell her. "I'm going to do some research on my computer to figure out the rest."

"What's a computer? Oh, and you told me you would show me what a flashlight was when we got back here, remember?"

She's so curious!

"Oh yeah!" I laugh and go to my bedside table and pull open a drawer and pull out my flashlight. "Here it is." I turn off my light, pull my curtains closed, and switch it on. Aurelia flies up and touches it exclaiming: "Oh!"

"Yeah, pretty cool little thing, isn't it? I use it for when power goes out at night or outside in the dark."

She nods and turns on her own purple glow. "I don't need a flashlight," she giggles. "Now what about this computer?"

"Right. Let's get to that," I say.

Aurelia plops down on her stomach on my desk, propping her chin on her hands and watches me pull up my favorite search engine.

I type in early enrollment for an art college in New York I've always wanted to attend and find what I hoped I would: they have a program that provides dual enrollment in high school and college.

This will be the perfect smokescreen for what I will really be doing: getting my high school diploma through an online school while I live in the Otherworld.

A quick search returns results for a couple of accredited online high schools that look good. I pick one at random when there aren't really any features to set one apart from another, and fill out the online application. I submit it and I'm in business!

Enroll in school. Check.

Then I send the information about the dual enrollment in the New York college to the printer.

Cover so I can be away from home and go to live in the Otherworld. Check.

"Dana," Mama calls up the stairs. "Dinner's ready!"

Figured it out in the nick of time.

I gather up the printed information and take it down to dinner with me.

Downstairs, my dad is waiting to greet me on the landing. "Hello, Dana!" he booms and pulls me into a hug. I'm what many would call a daddy's girl, and in my dad's arms my plan nearly fails right then and there.

Dad, I am going to go to school online and go live with a little man in the Otherworld so I can start learning how to be a Bard, but I'm going to lie to you and Mama and make you think I'm living at a college in New York, please forgive me and don't be mad at me for lying.

I could hear myself and see myself, run-on and all, blurting it all out in my head.

"Hi, Daddy! I missed you!"

"I missed you too" he says and kisses the top of my head.

We walk to the dining room with his arm around my shoulders and sit down to big plates of spaghetti and garlic bread. Mama looks at me expectantly. I know she wants me to make a really good case for what I want to do so that her decision is easy and she doesn't have to persuade my dad.

"Right, so Dad," I say giving them each a printed copy of the literature about the art college in New York. "I came up with an idea. You know I've been thinking of going to college in New York, right? Well, you can see here that the college I've been thinking of has a dual enrollment program with boarding options. This would make it possible to finish my high school degree in the same school where I'll go to college. Because I'm behind, they'll probably require that I go to school through the summer without a break, but I could finish and get out of this town. I won't have to worry about anything that's been making it so hard for me to go to school anymore." I say avoiding my dad's stare.

I almost wish this was really what I was going to do.

Mama looks at me with her face all screwed up into a frown. "I'm not sure you're ready for this, Dana."

'You mean you're not ready for this?' I think, nearly saying it aloud, but I know I can't be abrasive in this conversation.

I'm sure it will be hard for my parents to let me go. If I give them even the slightest indication that Mama is right, that I'm not mature enough for this, they'll both balk at the idea without giving it another thought.

"Mama, just think about it. While you do, I'm going to apply, okay?"

She looks distressed, but puts the papers aside and nods her head. I look at my dad and he is looking at me peculiarly.

What does that look mean, Dad?

"Well I'm proud of you, Dana. You're looking at your problems head-on trying to solve them. Part of this plan makes me feel like you're running from them a little, but it seems you've really thought this through and it might work out well for you. It makes me really happy that you don't want to just quit.

I'm interested to know more about the boarding situation for high school students, though. Can you get me some more information on that?" He smiles.

I smile too. *Yes! Dad's on my side!*

There's a lurch in my stomach at that moment. "Sure Dad!"

I'm pulling a fast one over on my parents and my Dad is proud of me? Ugh. It's hard to eat my dinner after that, but I do.

After dinner I clear the table and do the dishes the same as every night, then hug and kiss my parents good night, telling them I did a lot of hiking today and got really tired. I stomp up the stairs with heavy feet.

That part is true. I did hike a lot and I am tired.

When I get back to my room, Aurelia is on my desk, where she has been looking through my paintings and drawings waiting to hear how the presentation went.

"Well, what happened?" she asks.

"I presented it to them and they bought it all hook, line and sinker," I say, "but I don't feel very good about it. I feel rotten."

Aurelia can see that it is hard for me to lie to my parents. "I'm sorry, Dana. It's necessary right now, but it won't be forever. You'll see."

I smile at her weakly. "Thanks, Aurelia. I hope you're right. Tomorrow I have to get things moving and I just hope that it all goes well."

I pull back my sheets and blankets and crawl in. When I lay down Aurelia flies over and nestles into my collar settling down to sleep, and I have the most blissful night's sleep I've had in a long time.

CHAPTER FOUR

Forward Motion

My eyes fly open with the sunrise and I sit straight up.

Today I'm taking the first step to starting my life! I can't even believe it.

I hop happily out of bed and go to my computer where I print out the application for the school in New York. I grab up a pen, twirling it between my fingers, and head down for breakfast with my parents.

"Morning, Dana." Mama says smiling. "You look good this morning."

"Thanks, Mama. Morning. Where's Daddy?"

"I'm here," he says groggily as he walks through the kitchen door, eyes half open with bags under them.

"Whoa, you okay, Dad?"

He shuffles to the coffee pot where Mama has already made a big pot. "Yeah, I'm alright. Just didn't sleep well. I had some crazy dreams last night. They're hard to remember, but I know they were weird."

"Huh. Well sorry, Daddy."

He pulls a mug out of the cabinet and after pouring a cup he holds it out toward me and asks: "Want some?"

"Nah, I'm fine. I think you need it more than I do." I say chuckling.

I eat my daily bowl of cereal and shove my bowl out of the way pulling my application toward me. I start filling it out with my parents looking on. They smile at me when they see what I'm up to.

"Going to send that out today?" Mama asks.

"Yes ma'am. Do we have a big envelope and stamps?"

"Mm-hmm," she says with her coffee mug at her lips through a sip of coffee. "In the bureau drawer in the living room you'll find both."

I jump up to put my bowl in the washer and run out of the room with my application in hand. "Thanks!" I yell over my shoulder.

I'm so excited you would think I am actually doing this for real.

I finish filling it out and put my application in a big manila envelope. I address it, put about four stamps on just for good measure, and leave it on the hall table so they'll see it all ready to go, then back to the kitchen to pack another lunch.

After washing up and dressing I put my computer, my sketch pad, blanket and lunch in my backpack and get Aurelia situated in her mesh pocket.

I pull my beautiful key out of the pocket of my jeans from yesterday and put it on a cord I found in my jewelry box, then pull the cord over my head and drop the key down into my shirt.

It'll make a pretty cool necklace.

Just as I get to the bottom stair, I see my dad heading out the door with my envelope!

"Hey Dad, I got that." I say.

"Are you sure? I thought I could drop it in a mailbox for you."

"Oh yeah, I'm fine. I'm going to walk to the post office and then to school to withdraw myself."

"Well okay. Want a ride to the post office at least?" He asks.

I'd better take it.

I grin at him and bat my eyelashes. "Thanks, Daddy!"

He smiles at me, kisses my forehead, and turns to walk out the door.

Works every time.

"Bye, Mama!" I yell closing the door behind me.

I hop in the car with my dad and put my backpack carefully on the floor at my feet holding my envelope in my lap.

My dad cranks the engine and pulls out of the driveway.

"What are you up to, Dana?" he asks.

Uh-oh . . . Busted?

"What do you mean, Dad?"

"Dana, you've got that look you get when you're up to something."

"What? What look?" I can hear my voice go a little too high.

Calm own, Dana. Get a grip, or you're through.

"That one," he says pointing at my face. I force an exasperated sigh and roll my eyes at him.

"C'mon, Dad! I'm just excited! You know I don't really want to leave you and Mama, but after everything that's happened this is my chance to get out of here and start over somewhere new. It's my chance to get over it all."

"Okay, D. I know, I know. I get it," he relents. "I am proud of you."

"I know, Daddy, thank you. I'm pretty excited about this."

Ha! It's easy to be believable when you're telling the truth.

We pull up to the post office and I give him a kiss on the cheek. "Thanks for the ride, Daddy."

"You're welcome. Have a good day, Sweet Pea."

I get out with my backpack and my envelope and close the door, waving to my dad as he pulls away. This moment is both liberating and saddening at the same time. I can feel the door closing on this chapter of my life a little more every day.

How many more times will I get to do that?

I sigh and walk into the post office, head to the mail slots and pull one of the handles down opening a bin. I pretend to put something in at the same time tucking my envelope under my shirt as sneakily as possible in case someone sees me. We live in a pretty small town. If it gets back to my parents that someone saw me at the post office, I want it to also get back to them that I actually mailed something.

Now for the moment I've been looking forward to since the first day of the school year.

When I walk out of the post office and turn in the direction of my school, excitement really starts to build. It's impossible to count how many times this year I've wished I never had to go back to school again, and after today I won't. My sights are set on my new life as my feet carry me in the direction of the school.

The withdrawal process goes smoothly and I walk away without ever even looking back.

I won't be missing that place at all. My parents? Yes. School? Never. Bye-bye school! I won't be seeing you . . .

When I finally make it to a place where I can, I set my backpack down gently and check my pocket.

"Aurelia, are you ok in there?" I whisper.

"Yes, but I'm so ready to get out!" She chirps back.

"Okay, let's go see Séamus. What do you say?" I ask her.

"Yeah! Let's go!"

I look around us for a good, out-of-the-way place to sit so I can draw us over to the Otherworld. After a block or two I spot an alley and duck inside. There's a big air conditioning unit snug against one of the buildings and I decide that it will make a perfect shield for me to use while I prepare.

I wedge myself into the corner the unit makes with the building and I quickly sketch Séamus's cottage, (I've learned not to waste too much time on these transport drawings since they'll just disappear as soon as I use them anyway), singing one of the stronger songs he taught me so that I can transport directly to his house. As usual, the lines start trying to pop off the page and I close my eyes.

When I open them again I'm in the cool forest and the cottage is directly in front of me. I set my backpack down and pull open the pocket for Aurelia and she zooms out, flying a couple circles around the house.

"Woohoo!" She calls out as she rounds a corner to the back and I start laughing.

Poor faerie. She has been in that tiny pocket all day so far. I've got to think of a better way for her to travel with me.

When she calms down we approach Séamus's door and knock lightly.

He comes to the door shouting greetings to us before he even gets it open.

"Oh, hello, my young ones! You've come back ta see ole Séamus! So glad ta see you so soon! I thought it would be a while before I saw you again." He beckons us into his warm, cozy home. The fire is roaring in the hearth and the furry rug looks so welcoming. I head straight for it and flop down and Aurelia perches on my shoulder.

"We've got great news, Séamus!" Aurelia blurts out forgetting he can't understand her. The chirping she directs at him confuses him and he looks at me questioningly. I translate for her.

"Oh, have you now?" he asks as he settles onto a bench next to the rug in front of the hearth.

I nod. "I've worked out a plan to come and stay after Christmas is over in the Human World."

"That is good news!" he says beaming at me. "How'd you do it, then?"

"To make a long story short, I'm letting my parents think I'm going away to school for a long while, but I will really be here. The thing is I will need to do my school lessons while I'm here too and I'll have to pop over to the human world to connect my computer to the internet once a week so I can turn in my work. Do you think that will be okay?"

"Well, I think that'll be just fine," he says.

"Okay, we have a deal then. I'm getting excited to start learning everything I need to know." I say, my eyelids beginning to droop. The warmth from the fire, the luxury of the soft fur I am laying on, and the day's events all swirl together to form a cocktail of equal parts relief and exhaustion.

"Séamus, I'm getting so sleepy." I say.

"Well, close yer eyes. Take a bit of a rest." They're closing before he even finishes this sentence and before I even know I've gone to sleep, Aurelia is shaking and shaking me chirping in my ear.

"Dana, wake up. It's time to go! It's getting dark and

we need to get you home!"

My eyes flutter open reluctantly and I see Séamus sitting in a chair whittling something out of a piece of wood.

"Séamus, I'm so sorry. I slept nearly our whole visit!"

"Ah, it's just fine, Dana! Don't you worry yerself over it, now." He says smiling at me kindly. "You've had yerself a big day. Get home to yer family and enjoy the holidays with them."

"I will! Thanks for everything Séamus!" With that I pull out my sketchbook and sketch the back of my house and the big Camelia bush that grows next to it. I'm going to take a risk and go straight home.

Singing the song I close my eyes and when I open them again, I'm there lying on the grass behind our Camelia bush as if I was lying on the furry rug at Séamus's house.

Aurelia dives into my backpack pocket and under the cover of darkness I duck out of the shadows onto the sidewalk and walk calmly up to my front door.

CHAPTER FIVE

The Trip & the Watcher

The next few weeks pass with a blur. I get my dad all the information he could ever want about housing, and my parents are satisfied that I'll be living in a good place. The high school dorms at the college have constant supervision in the form of round-the-clock 'floor mothers', (graduate students who pay part of their tuition by teaching and part by busting boys trying to sneak into the girls' dorm).

Thanksgiving comes and goes and I visit the Otherworld several more times to do some more training with Séamus and a bit more exploring in the forest with Aurelia. Learning the Bard songs comes easily for me and our stout little friend tells me on several occasions what a "bloody fine Bard" I'm "turnin' into!".

Around the first week of December I wake up feeling like a girl on fire.

"Today's the day!" I say to Aurelia.

She looks at me with a look very similar to her angry face: eyebrows knitted together, face screwed up into a scowl. Her mouth doesn't frown however, it twists into something more like a smirk. "What day?"

"We've got to mail my acceptance and reward letters."

"Okay, well what's so great about that?" she asks.

"They have to be mailed from New York." I wink at her and smile and her whole face rearranges into a wide-eyed, beaming look of excitement.

"Oh I do love an adventure!" she exclaims.

"Now we just have to do a little scouting online and find a good place to pop into somewhere near a post office in the vicinity of the college."

I pull out my computer and get it booting up. Aurelia sits patiently next to it on the desk. She has gotten proficient fast, and knows her way around the internet already.

"You go down and have breakfast like normal, I'll look up post offices in the city near the college." she says.

"Awesome! Thanks Aury!"

I make an effort to calm myself. Today is a big day for me, but my parents definitely don't need to know it.

In the kitchen Mama is nibbling at her plate of eggs and bacon and sipping coffee.

"Morning, Mama. What's with the big breakfast?" I ask, playfully touching her forehead with the back of my hand as if checking for a fever.

"Ha ha ha. Very funny," she replies. "I just felt like cooking a good breakfast for my girl this morning."

"Well. Guess I'll have to eat it then. Can't have it going to waste, now can we?" I stick my tongue out in her direction. "Dad gone already?"

"Yeah, he left about 30 minutes ago."

"Have you checked the mail lately, Mama? Kind of hoped I would have heard back from the College by now," I say in the most authentic disappointed voice I can muster.

Mama's face brightens. "Oh, it has been a little while, hasn't it?" she smiles. "I'm sure something will be coming any day now," she seems to drift off somewhere, " . . . It's hard to believe you're going to be leaving and going so far away."

Yeah . . . far doesn't even begin to describe it.

"I hope it comes soon. I don't really like things being unresolved, without a solid plan in place. Not when it comes to school and my future, you know?"

She finishes eating and gets up to take her dishes to the sink. She stops and kisses the top of my head on the way by.

"You've always been a planner, D. I love you and I'm proud of you."

"Thanks, Mama."

Pretty sure you wouldn't be so proud if you knew what was really going on. Or then again, maybe you would. Why doesn't it feel as rotten to lie to you as it does Dad?

"By the way, Mom, I'm just going to stay in this morning and do some painting upstairs, okay?"

"Sure, Dana. I'll just be down here working. I have some billing to do for Dad."

"Okay."

She heads into the dining room to get started on work and I do my daily dishes ritual and head back upstairs.

When I get back to my desk Aurelia has mapped every post office in New York City. I chuckle in amazement. It's a bit funny to watch her type. She skips across the keys like she's landing on flowers in a field and the light from the computer screen lights up the front of her body and makes her wings sparkle like iridescent glass.

How did my life suddenly get so cool?

"Let's see," I say easing into my desk chair. "What do we have near the college?"

I take a look at what Aurelia has mapped and there are three post offices within walking distance of the college.

"Ok, now we need to do some scouting in the area."

When I drag the little man icon onto one of the streets on the map and the map changes to the street view, Aurelia jumps up and down and touches the computer screen.

"It's like a window! That is very strong magic!"

I can't hold back a giggle. "It's not magic, Aury. Trucks traveled all over the world taking pictures of the view from the street and this company pieced them all together in a computer program to make the picture you see when you put the little figure into the map. Not magic, just technology."

"Oh." she says, her smile drooping with disappointment.

"Technology isn't so bad. Today it's going to help us a lot. Being able to see New York this way first will give me an idea of where we can pop into there without being seen."

"Still, not as good as magic," she says.

"Look there." I point to a place between two big buildings in the street view, "It's a tiny alley with some dumpsters. It's probably going to be pretty gross, but let's pop in between them. We should be able to get in there pretty quietly."

"Ok," she says. "That sounds like a good idea."

"Now I'll just print the map so we can get around pretty easily once we get there. Oh! I almost forgot! I need to grab the College's logo too. I still have to make the letters."

I type two letters from the College, agonizing over details like business letter headings and addresses, spelling, punctuation and grammar. One is an acceptance letter and the other states that I've been awarded a full scholarship.

Can't have my parents sending money to pay a tuition for a student that isn't even enrolled!

I finish printing the letters and envelopes and get them stamped and ready to go.

"I'll be back soon," I say. "I'm going to go down and pack some food and snacks for the trip."

I run downstairs to the kitchen.

"We . . . I'm going to go out for a bit, Mama," I yell as I run by the dinning room.

Almost said we're going to go out! Crap!

I grab lunch, some fruit and a couple of water bottles, and go back upstairs to pack my backpack. Aurelia slips into her pocket and I run down to the dinning room.

"See you a little later on, Mama." I smile and kiss her cheek and she doesn't really look up from her work.

"Crazy number crunching going on today, huh?"

"Oh hi, Dana. What . . . ?" she says like she just realized I was there.

"Nothing, Mama. I'll be home a little after dark tonight probably. Love you."

"Oh, okay, D. I love you too."

The trip to the park goes pretty quickly. I can't wait to try transporting to New York since I haven't transported anywhere in the human world yet.

Probably should have tried some smaller jumps first to practice . . . but whatever! It's pretty amazing that in a just a few minutes I will be in New York!

I make it to the wall and duck inside quickly. I don't want to waste any time today. Aurelia frees herself from her little pocket while I take out my blanket, sketchbook and pencils.

"I'm a little nervous, Aury," I say. "What if something goes wrong?"

She flies up and kisses my cheek and her faerie calm washes over me.

"You're so good at that!" I say smiling at her.

"You're going to do just fine, Dana! Don't worry!"

"Okay, well let's get to it."

I sit down on the blanket, prop my sketchbook on my backpack and set to work drawing the two dumpsters in the dirty alley. While I draw I see myself sitting between them, thinking of where they are located in the city. I start singing the most powerful Bard Song Séamus has taught me so far. He says it should work, but I'm so nervous my voice is shaky and it sounds pretty bad.

Aurelia flies over and sits on my shoulder and nuzzles into my hair. She's like a father's hands on the bicycle seat when you're learning to ride. I feel invincible like I can't possibly fall down.

Soon the lines on the page start to pop and Aurelia claps her hands where she sits on my shoulder. It's time.

I close my eyes until the most awful odor I've ever smelled in my life accosts my nostrils. It's like a mix of putrid garbage, a nasty bathroom that has never been cleaned, and diesel fuel.

"Ugh!" I open my eyes and we are in the alley. I'm still sitting on my blanket, thank goodness. Who knows what's under it!

A feeling of great accomplishment rushes in and

crowds out disgust instantly. I'm smiling smugly to myself.

"Aurelia! I did it!"

"I knew you could!" she says. She has flown down from my shoulder to jump up and down on my backpack in front of me, clapping and cheering.

I stand up and look around.

Now I just need to get my bearing.

I pull out the map and take a look at it. The route to the post office is fairly short. The trip there should be a quick one. I gather up my backpack and grab the corner of the blanket, then reconsider, frowning in disgust once again.

"I think I'll just leave that here." I say. "Maybe someone who really needs it will find it and use it."

"Good idea," Aurelia replies then slips into my backpack pocket.

And away we go!

I step out of the alley and I'm struck by the lack of green. There are no trees or flowers anywhere! And so many people! It's not like I didn't know New York has millions of people, it's just really hard to imagine until you see it for yourself.

I'm no stranger to the city, but my city is much different from this. In Atlanta there are trees planted in little holes in the sidewalks on most every street. I can't see a spot of green in any direction in New York.

Okay, focus, Dana. You're on a mission here. Get this done and then you can marvel at the concrete jungle.

I start walking in the direction I need to go to get to the post office, but I only take a few steps in the crowd when I get sandwiched between someone walking the same direction I am on my right, and someone walking the opposite direction on my left. My shoulder slams kind of hard into the woman on my left as we meet and she gets angry. She spins around to face me and throws her hands up, palms up and yells at me.

I'm so mortified I don't even know what she says.

"I'm sorry," I say shrugging, feeling like I've shrunk to Aurelia's size. "I didn't mean to." She gives me the middle finger and turns and walks away.

Man, these people are nuts.

"You okay back there?" I whisper to Aurelia, hoping she's not getting smashed.

"Yeah," she squeaks back.

A brisk, but careful, five-minute walk brings us to the post office entrance. I walk inside, pull my letters out of my backpack, and double-check that everything is right:

Address: check.

Stamps: check.

Biggest lie of my life: check!

Feeling like a total fraud, I drop them in the slot, but then I remember why I'm doing all of this and I immediately feel better.

Walking out of the post office, I notice that the world looks different. I'm not a child anymore and I'm no longer seeing it through a child's eyes. Things look smaller, dirtier, and definitely harder, but I feel tough and a little more ready for new paths and new adventures. I would be lying to myself if I didn't admit that I'm also a wee bit scared of what lies ahead. I'm taking a step in a direction I can never turn back from. Everything is going to change.

Everything has already changed, I remind myself. *Nothing has been the same since the ordeal. That one day changed my life forever.*

I continue to stand and look at the buildings and the people, lost in my inner dialogue.

"Is everything okay?" I hear from Aurelia's pocket.

"Mmm-hmm." I mumble, but I still don't move. I just need to take it in and make peace with the tumult.

The feelings I'm having are so overwhelming. It's like happiness and sadness at the same time; like fear and bravery. When two such opposite feelings are rolling around inside a person at once it feels like a battle. One feeling surges and pushes down the other and then the tides change and the other feeling rises up for a bit. It's almost maddening to be so split inside.

As my head begins to clear, I realize people are staring at me just standing and looking around.

I must look like such a tourist!

Then I resign myself.

Well so what? I am. Might as well make the best of the rest of the day.

I sit down on a nearby bench and pull my backpack into my lap. I pull open Aurelia's pocket and look in on her. She gives me a thumbs up and I smile, amused at how modern my ancient faerie is becoming.

She must have learned to do that on my social media sites.

I pull out my map and look up the Met. I've always wanted to see the Metropolitan Museum of Art, and now's my chance!

Maybe I'll come back a few times before I have to go to the Otherworld to stay.

That thought makes me happy. The freedom of being able to transport like this is a dream come true. I could go to Paris, Rome, Greece; all the places I've ever wanted to see! The sky's the limit!

Changing my focus to the excitement of the possibility

of seeing some of the most amazing sights in the world has me feeling better. I hop up off the bench and put my backpack on, heading toward the museum with a renewed skip in my step.

What a fantastic day!

When I arrive at the front steps of the Met, I'm awe struck. I stand still again, looking at the giant building. The huge banners hanging from its facade make me think of a lovely Greek woman draped in flowing togas. The dozen or so crows perched on various parts of the building are her pets. *Everything about this day feels magical.*

Eager to get inside to see all the fantastic art, I start up the steps, skipping a couple along the way. I flash my student ID to one of the attendants taking admission payments from visitors and she hands me a map of the Met, waving me through.

"Whew. I wondered for a minute if I would be able to get in with no money." I mumble back to Aurelia. I open the map of the museum and study it, pondering where best to start. This place is so big there's no way I could ever get through it in a day, much less the few hours I can spend today. I will definitely be coming back.

When I look up from the map there is a man standing against the opposite wall looking at me. I nod to him smiling. He smiles back. He's dressed a little oddly, but I suppose things are different here in the city.

Aurelia and I start on our way, stopping to look at the incredible works of art. I make sure I turn sideways for a few minutes at some paintings, and pretend to look further down in the giant rooms to decide which way I want to go. What I am really doing is giving Aurelia a chance to study the paintings I particularly like. Since her pocket is on the side of my backpack it would be hard for her to see a painting I am looking at without peeking out.

"What do you think?" I whisper back to her.

"I think these paintings are not as lucky as I am. They weren't painted by Bards so they could come to life . . ." I laugh, but deep down I feel pretty proud at that moment.

I round a corner turning into another room and the same oddly-dressed man is there watching me. Again he smiles at me and walks past me to the room I just came from.

Weird guy.

I walk and walk, trying to get through as many rooms as I can in one day. It seems like I walk for miles, stopping, looking at a painting, moving on to another. I come to a painting called 'Young Woman Drawing' and I am struck by how powerful it is. The 'Young Woman' sits in front of a window, light flooding into an otherwise dimly lit room. She wears a flowing white gown with a pink sash and holds a large drawing board on her lap that she has been using. She looks out of the painting at the viewer. Her expression is very hard to read. She looks sort of sad, but it's hard to tell. Maybe she's just caught off guard in a moment of deep concentration. The light reflects off her paper in front of her and lights up her face exaggerating her features, somehow making her look even more mysterious.

I think I'll sketch this, I think as I sit down on one of the benches in the center of the room and put my backpack down on the floor in front of me so that Aurelia can face the painting. Then I carefully pull out my sketchbook and some charcoal.

"Just be sure you don't sing or hum, Dana." Aurelia squeaks while I'm bent over my backpack.

I laugh and whisper back.

"I'll try."

Sketching the painting doesn't take very long. It's somewhat hard to recreate the lighting without color, but I finally get the drawing to a point of completion that I'm happy with, and close my sketchbook back up and tuck it away inside my backpack. As I'm preparing to move on to the next room, I look up and the same man is watching me again.

Okay, this is getting a little creepy. I think it might be time to go.

"Aurelia, something is up with that guy watching me over there. I've seen him a few times now. I'm going to walk back to the same alley we popped into and head home, okay?"

"Okay." she says, sounding nervous.

I tighten up my backpack straps significantly so that I can walk quickly without the bag bouncing up and down, then I take off.

I'm settling into a good steady pace dodging art spectators in the museum, and I've almost made it back to the front entrance when I see him again. He is leaned against an archway like he is waiting for me!

What the . . .

I don't look at him. I walk by looking straight ahead toward the doors barely making it to the entrance before breaking into a full out sprint, bursting through the doors out onto the stairs, nearly stumbling on my way down. The sidewalk is full of people.

I glance back.

"He's chasing us! What should I do?"

"Just keep running!" Aurelia yells.

So I do. I'm running scared. I don't care who I hit or how many don't walk signs I run through. I stop just for a second at a crosswalk where there are cars in the intersection. So I cross the other street and by the time I get to the other side the crosswalk in the direction I'm going is free.

"Dana, get your sketchbook out and start drawing home."

"How the hell am I going to run for my life and draw at the same time?" I yell.

"You'll just have to take little breaks to stop for a second. The drawings don't have to be perfect."

"Okay," I huff doubtfully.

I stop and look back. He's not as good at dodging people in crowds, so he's a good distance behind me. I jerk my sketchbook out of my backpack and start drawing the Camelia bush in my back yard again.

He's beginning to close the gap, so I take off running again, with my sketchbook tucked under one arm, pencil in hand like a weapon.

People are shouting at both of us. Obscenities are flying left and right. I glance back and see a man try to stop him.

"Hey man! Leave her alone! What the hell are you doing? I'm calling the Po . . ." he trails off as I get out of range.

I spot an alley just ahead that hopefully will serve as a good transport spot out of the way so people don't see me disappear. I can't remember how to get back to the alley we popped into and there's no time to figure it out.

As I get closer to the alley, over my shoulder I see that he has gained a little ground, so I know I've got to do something fast! When I duck into the alley I immediately take a knee and sketch wildly.

"I think I'd better use this alley! I don't think we'll

make it back to the one we came from without being caught!" I stammer between gasps.

I'm trying to sing, but my voice is so shaky from fear that nothing is really coming out.

Get it together, Dana!

Just as he tears around the corner into the alley I find my voice and see the lines of the drawing begin to pop. Aurelia wriggles free of her pocket and flies at him like a lightening bolt! Just as he comes within approximately ten feet of me she circles his head once and he swats at her like a fly. As I am closing my eyes the light glints off something on his hand: a large insignia ring with a cross on it.

Then my eyes close and I am home.

I collapse in a heap, panting hard and grateful to be safe.

I'm home . . . thank God, I'm home.

I take a minute to kneel there trying to catch my breath and calm down. My heart is pounding out of my chest and I'm huffing and puffing.

Aurelia.

My eyes start to well with tears.

I had to leave her. If I had waited and that guy had touched me as I started to transport he would be here with me now.

She saved me.

I stand up and walk around the side of my house to the front sidewalk staring at the ground out, of my mind with worry.

"Dana," I jump and gasp, looking up just in time to see my dad close his car door and walk up to the side walk. "What in the world were you doing back there?"

"Oh. Hi Dad." I can only force half a smile. "I was on

my way home from the park and I thought I heard something back there. It was just a stray cat. I shooed it away."

"Good. Damn feral cats are such a menace."

"Yeah," I say as we walk up the front steps to the door. "Hey Dad, I don't really feel very hungry. I've had a long day. I think I am just going to go upstairs and read in bed. Is that okay?"

There's no way I can act for you and Mama tonight.

"Well, sure, Honey. That's fine."

We walk through the font door and Mama looks up at us from her reading chair in the living room.

"Dana's going to go on to bed. She says she's not hungry."

"Oh? D, you okay?"

I'm already about half way up the stairs. "Yeah, Mama, I'm fine. Just don't really feel like dinner." I say, steadily climbing the stairs.

I get to my room and go in closing the door behind me, knees buckling with the click of the door latch. The weight of everything that has happened in the last hours mixes with feelings that always seem to bubble just under the surface of my life since last Spring, and my body goes limp. I sit down on the floor hard and my back slides down the door until my head rests on the carpet because it's so heavy I can no longer hold it up.

Despair fills my heart like water in a cup that runs over. It wells up in my eyes and spills over my lids. I'm drowning in it and my sobs are gasps - great gulps I take trying to get to the surface of my grief.

I'm grieving for my body, for my stolen dignity, for my friend Aurelia, whom I've lost tonight. I'm grieving for my self-love and for my innocence. My world is black, and nothing seems to make any sense. Nothing will ever be the same.

After what feels like hours of wracking sobs, my tears dry up and I sink into sleep like sinking to the bottom of a lake, the blackness overtaking me like water seeping into my lungs.

CHAPTER SIX

Puzzle Pieces

The night is quiet. The sounds of my feet pounding on the cobblestones echo off the buildings around me. There are no lights anywhere, so I'm relying only on moonlight to light my way. The buildings are so weird, not that I have a lot of time to study them while I'm running as fast as my feet can carry me.

I'm hurtling myself forward, trying to find a place, anywhere I can feel safe, running blindly.

Where am I?

I feel panicked. He's not far behind me and gaining ground with every step.

Up ahead I can see the outline of a huge building looming over everything else in the town. It's a church.

I scramble up the steps, throw open the doors, and the scene changes. I stop in my tracks when I see . . . myself?

I see myself sprawled out on the floor just in front of the altar thrashing and flailing trying to get away from him. I run toward the me that's struggling and watch the scene unfold as if watching a movie clip in slow motion.

The man standing over that version of me wears a

66

white tunic with a red cross on the back and a metal helmet. He jerks a knife out of its sheaf at his hip and raises it over his head.

At the same time another man rushes past me in the aisle.

"Wait!" he screams.

I am within twenty yards of the scene unfolding at the altar and the running man is even closer, when the helmeted murderer plunges his knife into the chest of the me on the floor and pulls it back out promptly. I can smell the blood that immediately begins flowing from my chest. He drops the knife and when he does I see the familiar gold ring with a cross stamped into it on his finger.

The me on the floor gasps for air and then I am her, no longer two of me, only one - dying on the floor of a church in a place I've never been. I don't know where I am or what I'm doing here.

Who will tell my parents what happened to me? They will be left to wonder where I went for the rest of their lives.

Suddenly another face is standing over me, the man from New York. His eyes are red and puffy, brimming with tears. His face contorts into a sob and he calls out an order to someone else.

"Hurry! You've got to hurry. She needs us now!"

My chest burns like it's on fire, but cold is spreading through the rest of my body. My eyelids are heavy.

I'll just take a short nap and then I'll get up and go find help . . .

When I finally close my eyes there is only black. I don't think or feel, I just am. There is no floor beneath me, no roof above me, no sky overhead. There is only infinity.

I open my eyes, and I'm laying in my bed wearing my pajamas. My heart jumps up in my throat when I notice the spot of purple on my extra pillow.

Aurelia!

"Aury! You're here! Are you ok?"

She rouses wearily and blinks away sleep.

"I'm sorry I worried you," she starts, "After that man came after you I needed to see Merlin. You're in danger now and I'm not sure I will be able to protect you always."

"I know, I think you're right. I had a dream about that crazy guy last night. He was wearing different clothes and actually killed me! Then he showed up in the same clothes he wore in New York, standing over me. I don't understand what it all means. I'm really confused." Panic starts to rise up, words tumbling out of my mouth faster and faster. "Aury, it wasn't like a dream, it was like the first few times I was in the Otherworld and only thought I was dreaming. I even felt myself die and what it was like after my body was dead!"

Aurelia looked down shaking her head. "I can't give you the answers to this either. Merlin was insistent that we need to get you to the Otherworld to stay as soon as possible. You'll be safe there. You'll be able to talk to people that can help you."

"I know, but we have to wait for the letters to come. There's nothing I can do until after that happens. In the meantime, can I go talk to Merlin? Do you think he might be able to tell me anything about the man in New York?"

"No, Merlin says it's important that you find some answers on your own. It's supposed to help you grow as a

Bard."

"Okay then, what about Séamus? Think he might have some information that can help me?"

"I don't know," she says and I notice that she isn't smiling. She's not as playful and animated as usual.

"Are you sure everything is okay, Aurelia? You don't seem like yourself."

She winces as she turns around. One of her wings is badly damaged. "Oh Aury!" My voice cracks. "What do I do?"

Her face looks so sad and she can't look at me. She shakes her head slowly.

"When a faerie's wings are damaged she dies, just like a butterfly. There's nothing that can help."

"No . . ." I gasp, and suddenly the unthinkable happens: my black world gets even darker.

What can I do? I thought I had lost her, and I get her back for what? To lose her again? I can't even search this on the internet . . . she's probably the only one of her kind. Could someone in the Otherworld help her?

My mind is going over every possible solution, racing through everything I know and remembering everything I have learned so recently. My eyes fall on my desk, zeroing in on my sketchbook and the pencil sitting on top.

"Aury," I say quietly, still mulling it over. "I have an idea . . . First I need to go through the motions of my morning routine. I was so upset last night I went straight to bed. If I don't show up downstairs for breakfast my parents will think something is up. While I'm downstairs you get some more rest. Is there anything you need right now before I go?"

"No, I think I am just going to sleep a while longer."

"Okay, I'll hurry." I kiss the tip of my index finger and touch it to the top of her head. She smiles weakly and gathers a bit of the loose pillow case pulling it up over her body to her chin.

I turn toward my door and plaster on the best fake smile I can muster for the outside world while my insides are churning. I hate doing it, but I am an expert. The occasion to wear a false smile happens at least once every day. Today it's a lot more difficult than usual because Aurelia's injury is a big distraction. It weighs on my mind and causes me to falter a couple of times while I'm in the kitchen with my parents.

"Hi, Mama. Sleep okay?"

"Well, kind of. I would have slept a lot better if you had come home and eaten dinner with us like normal last night. Is everything alright?" The concerned frown distorts her face.

"I'm fine! I was just tired, that's all. No biggie." I say between hurried bites of my favorite cereal.

"Good grief, Dana. What's the rush? Slow down!"

Act natural, be normal . . .

"Sorry, Mama. I just want to get outside again today. It won't be long before the weather starts getting cold."

I jump up and head for the stairs.

"Uh, D?"

"Yeah, Mama?"

"Aren't you forgetting something?"

"Oh! Pfft! Sorry, I've got a lot on my mind, I totally spaced it!" I smile at her and shrug as I walk back to the counter to get my bowl, rinse it, and put it in the dishwasher.

When I turn back to the door heading for the stairs I hold my breath and squeeze my eyes shut, waiting for

Mama to say something else. She doesn't and I exhale a giant sigh and run up the stairs two-at-a-time.

In my room Aurelia is still asleep on her pillow.

I've got to hurry.

I get my backpack all set to go, packing sketchbooks and pencils, a set of extra clothes, my toothbrush - everything I'll need for an overnight stay. It's a Friday and I have a plan. I go to Aurelia's pillow bed and gently wake her.

"Aurelia . . ." I whisper. "We need to get going now."

She barely opens her eyes and doesn't say anything, only nods half-heartedly.

Oh no.

I scoop her up gingerly and hold her on my palm.

"No backpack pocket for you today, Aury."

This is going to be tricky.

At the top of the stairs I crouch low to make sure no one is at the bottom before I start down. I take every step as quietly as possible and as soon as I get to a point where I can, I peer back toward the kitchen and look to the doorways for the living room and dining room. I can see Mama sitting in her reading chair, but it doesn't seem that Dad is anywhere around.

Hmm, he wasn't at breakfast either. He must be out of town today . . . that makes things a bit easier.

At the bottom of the stairs I switch Aurelia to my left hand and walk very quietly toward Mama. I don't want her to look up before I'm at the living room doorway.

Whew! She didn't.

I lean my left shoulder on the left side of the door frame, kind of leaning around the door jamb into the room with my right shoulder keeping Aurelia out of sight that way.

"Mama, a couple of the girls from school - you remember Ella and Taylor? They want to have a sleep over this weekend. It might be the last time I can for a while if I get into the college. Is that okay with you?"

"Well sure. Be home tomorrow?"

"I was thinking Sunday . . . ?

"I guess that's okay. Just behave yourself."

"Of course I will, Mama! Jeez." I roll my eyes for effect.

Yes! I'm free!

I tuck Aurelia behind my back and walk further in to kiss Mama on the cheek and thankfully she doesn't notice that I'm hiding something. I smile and take a step or two back out of the room, duck behind the wall and head to the kitchen.

"I'm just going to get a few snacks to take with me!" I call out to her.

I grab a couple granola bars and some bottled waters and tuck them into my backpack, which is pretty hard to do with one hand, then make a run for the door.

"Bye, Mama. See you Sunday!" I yell. By the time I get to the word Sunday, the door has already slammed and my feet are already pounding the pavement.

I carry Aurelia like a football while I sprint to the park. Trying to be gentle with her while I'm running is difficult. Unlike a football, she's a living being and I don't want to cause anymore damage than she already has.

I get to the park in record time. I run and run - all the way to the wall, ducking into the secret room in one fluid motion.

Once inside I immediately sit down with my legs out in front of me and lay Aurelia carefully on my lap, pull out my sketchbooks and start drawing her. I am singing the most powerful song I know so far at the top of my lungs, drawing her wings perfectly.

If she can't regrow the wing, and it can't be healed, then I'll draw her whole again . . .

My drawing is nearing completion quickly and it's looking pretty good when the lines begin to pop. I don't close my eyes this time because I want to see what happens and I can see them pop harder and harder until the drawing almost comes off the page completely, looking like a flat cartoon.

I try and try to keep my eyes open, but my eyelids get heavy until they finally close against my will for an instant. When I realize they have, I jerk them back open and I'm in the meadow.

I guess it's like a sneeze, impossible to keep your eyes open through.

My sketchbook page is blank.

A good sign! Something happened.

I toss my sketchbook aside and turn my attention to Aurelia. I nudge her carefully with the tip of my index finger, and she rouses from sleep, looking up at me. Her eyes open wide and she sits up, seemingly taking stock of where she is and how her body feels.

"Did it work?" I ask her expectantly, but she doesn't say anything. She wraps her arms around herself and wiggles back and forth unfolding her wings and flapping them a few times. Her face brightens and she looks up at me. It's hard for me to tell, but they look normal, not broken.

"What did you do?" she looks so confused.

"I drew your wings whole again and we wound up here, as usual," I laugh.

A second later she rockets straight up in the air about

50 feet, arches her back and appears to do something like a backward swan dive. Just as she reaches the ground she straightens out and zooms across the field away from me. At the edge of the meadow she makes a u-turn and skims the top of the grasses in the field at lightening speed, then stops right in front of me with an armful of wildflowers. There's a huge smile plastered on her face.

She holds the flowers out to me dropping a couple of them.

"I love you, Dana. You saved my life!"

"You saved mine first," I say and wink at her taking the flowers. I pull a pony-tail-holder out of my backpack and loosely french-braid my long, thick hair, then tuck each one of Aurelia's flowers into my braid from top to bottom. I don't have a mirror, but I think it's probably pretty.

"Shall we?" I ask, standing up and lugging my backpack up hoisting it into its place on my back. I stand up straight feeling ten feet tall and pretty proud of myself, overjoyed that Aurelia is going to be alright.

We start on the walk to Séamus's house chit-chatting along the way when I suddenly realize that Aurelia doesn't know we can stay a couple of days this time!

"So guess what?"

She flies close and picks up the end of my braid playfully then drops it.

"What?" she asks obviously in as great a mood as I am.

"I worked it out so that we could stay a couple of days this visit!"

Aurelia flies out in front of my face and clasps her hands together in front of her, shrugging with excitement. "That's great!"

We step into the forest laughing, but as soon as we get completely under the cover of the trees I immediately sense something is wrong. There are huge crows peppering the treetops cawing and making a great deal of noise. The cacophony is deafening.

Aurelia's fear shows on her face and she races over to me, wraps a hand in my braid, standing steadfast on my shoulder. I'm not sure if she's shielding me or wanting me to shield her.

I quicken my pace when as Séamus's house comes into view. Dozens of crows are perched on his roof giving the scene a distinct horror film feel.

I run up to the door and am about to knock, but the door isn't latched. It's open a couple of inches, so instead I push slowly inching my head inside to peer into the blackness. The state of the cottage is utterly alarming.

The fire in the hearth has gone out and the contents of Séamus's little house are thrown around everywhere. Nothing is in it's place. Furniture is overturned, dishes are broken on the floor.

I step in quietly, on guard, scanning the room for intruders, and Aurelia flies up off my shoulder to get a better look.

"Séamus!" she yells as we spot him virtually at the same time. He is sprawled on the floor in his kitchen. I run to where he's laying in a pool of his own blood. His eyes are closed and he's covered in blood as well.

"What happened here?" I gasp. I feel for a pulse and he has one, but it's not very strong. I look him over, searching for the source of all the blood and find a few gaping cuts, mostly on his arms.

"Aury, we've got to get him some help! I can't do much for him." I look for some towels and find a few rags that I tear into strips. I clean him up as best as I can and tie the strips tightly around his wounds to help stop the bleeding. When we've got all his wounds covered, I pick him up and take him to the fur rug to try to make him comfortable. Now completely overwhelmed, I sit down, bury my head in my hands, and cry. Again.

"I don't know what to do," I say through my sobs.

"Oh, now young one, dry yer tears . . ." Séamus's voice is weak and he can barely make a sound. "I'll be okay."

"Séamus! What happened to you?"

"It was the Templars."

"The what?" I ask shaking my head. I don't know what Templars are, but I have a hunch.

"Was it a man wearing a white tunic with a red cross on it and a metal helmet? Was there a gold ring on his finger?"

"Yeah, that's a Templar, alright," he grunts, trying to sit up.

"I don't understand what's happening," I say slowly, the heaviness of the guilt over Aurelia's injury and now Séamus's making me feel very tired and hopeless. "First one of those guys chases me down, now you, Séamus? Why?"

"They're protecting the church. It's their job."

"Protecting the church?" I can feel my face screw up into a look of indignation. "Séamus! I think it's time someone gives me some answers! Don't you think? I mean, we're all being threatened. The same man that chased me down, and hurt Aurelia, has now come to the Otherworld, and from the looks of it, tried to kill you. Why is this happening?"

"Yer probably right. It's time." He points to a bookshelf on the wall opposite the fireplace. "There's a book up there that'll tell you a little, but not all. Can you do me a favor and get the fire going again first?"

"Oh, yeah. That's probably a good idea. It's kind of chilly in here." I walk outside to get wood and notice that all the crows have gone away.

I shake my head. *That's so weird. Crows, Templars, dying dreams. What the hell is going on?*

I walk back inside with an armload of chopped wood and set it up in the fireplace with some kindling, but I don't have a lighter. I look around the hearth and don't see one there either.

"Séamus, how do you light this?"

"With me mind," he chuckles. "You try."

"What? I can't light a fire with my mind!"

"Oh no? A few weeks ago you wouldn't have thought you could draw a faerie into being, or transport to another world, or to other places within yer own world would you?"

"Well . . . no. Of course I wouldn't have."

"And can you do those things now?"

"Yeah," I sigh, "I can."

"Get me point?"

I roll my eyes like I do at my parents before I even realize I'm doing it and then feel embarrassed. Thankfully I don't think he notices, or maybe doesn't know what it means.

"So how do I do this exactly, Séamus?"

"You just have to see it in yer mind. Meditate on it if you know what I mean."

"Not really . . . no." I say, exasperated.

I'm supposed to start my training with this guy? How am I ever going to learn anything?

"Close yer eyes, girl. Empty yer mind of everything.

All you see is the fireplace. It's empty and cold. Now see it with a roaring fire in. Open yer eyes and repeat the process with yer eyes open. It might help you to sing one of the simple songs."

"Okay, I'll try it," I say doubtfully.

I look at the hearth . . . and look, and look. I can't picture flames there. I turn to Séamus and look at him pleadingly.

"At this rate we'll never have a fire," I say.

"C'mon Dana, tune out the room. Its just you and the fireplace. Make it happen."

I sigh and turn my attention back to the fireplace decidedly more determined, and this time something odd happens.

It's like I'm looking through a camera's zoom. My gaze hones into the logs and the rest of the room disappears. After a moment I remember to sing and the melody of one of the first songs I learned pours out of my mouth like it's second nature. I don't even have to remember the tune, it's like I have always sung this song. I can see the flames growing on the logs. I watch them in my mind's eye for several minutes and suddenly the logs burst into flame. I'm so startled I stumble backward and fall down.

I laugh and look from Séamus to Aurelia who are both beaming at me.

"That's it!" Séamus says as emphatically as he can. He winces in pain.

"Séamus, take it easy. Tell me what I can do for you."

"Don't you worry about me, I'll be fine." He's so stubborn it's exasperating.

"Maybe you will, maybe you need some medical attention. What do we do if it starts looking like you'll need help healing up?"

"Actually, I'm not sure. Nothing like this has ever happened here before. No one is supposed to be able to be hurt here."

"I suppose I will just have to take you back to the human world in that case . . ." I say more to myself than to Séamus. I'm worried about this situation, because as it turns out, I'm not necessarily as safe here afterall, and neither are my friends.

Why do this to Séamus? Is this some kind of message to me?

I remember that I am supposed to be finding a book on the shelf. "What's the book I'm looking for, Séamus?"

"Right, the book. Look on the top shelf for a brown leather-bound book called 'Legends of the Celts'."

I locate it easily and bring it down, unleashing a torrent of dust motes that fly through the air and make me sneeze.

"Don't read this book often, Séamus?" I ask through sniffles.

He chuckles, grimacing. "Nah. No need ta read it much. I memorized it long ago as a wee boy, and I can tell you the story, but I think you need ta read it for yerself." He holds his hands out for the book and I hand it to him.

Yuck. I wipe the dust off my hands on my jeans leaving dirty streaks on the front of my legs.

Séamus thumbs through the pages seemingly looking for something specific.

"Here 'tis!" he exclaims, but moans in pain a little and shifts on the rug trying to get comfortable. "I keep forgetting to be careful," he mumbles as I settle in next to him to read this ancient looking book.

"Read this part here," Séamus says pointing to a short passage.

* * *

The gods tell of a day when, from another time and place the world's Savior shall come. Her manner of dress and speech shall be unlike anything we have known. She shall bear no weapons, save her voice, artistic skill, and the sacred key of life. The key is a gift to her directly from the Gods and only she may touch it.

She and her faerie companion will travel far and wide, throughout time to right wrongs that are in our future, as well as in our past. She shall be a Sage among the Druids.

Be ever watchful for the day the Savior shows herself. Be prepared to welcome her into your home, give her shelter and warmth, feed her. Offer her any assistance she may require, for her destiny is the destiny of our world. If she perishes, so shall we all, not just in our world, but all worlds.

I look at Séamus, narrowing my eyes in thought for several moments of silence, trying to decide what this is. I back away feeling angry and confused.

"Is this some kind of crazy joke, Séamus? What does this mean? Are you trying to tell me that I'm some kind of Savior?" My voice has gotten louder with every word until by the end of this sentence I am yelling.

"Calm down now." he says. "Do you have a key, then?"

Truthfully, I had almost forgotten about the key hanging around my neck. "Yes . . . I have a key, but what does that mean? Anyone can have a key!"

"How did you happen ta get this key?"

My thoughts go back to the strange circumstances surrounding the day at the wall. "I drew some symbols I saw on a stone block and then . . . they rearranged themselves into a smaller block . . . the key was . . . behind . . . " I shake my head. "What does that have to do with anything, Séamus?" I'm yelling again.

"Dana," he says calmly, "It came from the gods. The text says no one else can touch it. Get the key out." When I hesitate, the exasperation shows on his face and he waves me forward repeatedly, as if to say 'get on with it'.

Doubtfully I pull the cord I wear around my neck out of my shirt and the key dangles on the end.

Séamus's eyes light up when he sees it. "I never thought I'd see this day . . . Put it here near me so I can reach it."

I pull the cord over my head and untie it, taking the key off, and put the key on the wood floor next to the rug. I watch as he reaches out to touch it, and as his fingers get close, it moves slightly out of his reach.

He looks up at me with a huge grin, obviously encouraged.

"Slide it back here. I wanna have a go at it again."

I do as he asks and this time he reaches quickly for the key and as his fingers nearly touch it sparks fly between the key and his fingers and it goes sliding quickly across the floor to the other side of the room.

Oh my God. He can't touch it . . . He. can't. touch. it!

"Aurelia, will you try, please?" I ask her.

"I don't know," she says. She looks afraid.

"Okay, it's alright. You don't have to. I have another idea. Séamus, can I use you one more time? I am going to put the key directly into your hand . . . promise me you're not doing this."

"I promise." he says laughing weakly. "I wanna touch it!"

I shuffle across the floor to retrieve my key and I hold it in my hand above Séamus's. His palm is open, facing up ready for me to drop it.

I do and the sparks fly again, bigger and more violently this time and the key flies through the air across the room with an amazing amount of force, ricocheting off two walls before finally coming to land at my feet.

I stand and look down at it.

Now what? I am supposed to believe that I'm some Savior? That I'm going to save the world? I'm just Dana - no savior. Shouldn't a savior be pure or something? There is nothing good in me and certainly nothing pure. I'm about as dirty as a girl can get. I can't save the world!

A tear slips out of my eye and drops to the floor barely missing the key and I reach down to pick it up. I hold it close to my face and study it.

How can I be anything special?

I used to feel special before . . . it happened . . . but not now. Now I can't feel anything but cold and dark.

I'm not special. I'm not a savior.

"There's been some mistake, Séamus. I'm not who you think I am. I'm not who your people think I am. There's nothing I can do for you." With that I turn and walk out the door.

Outside when Aurelia tries to follow I hold my hand out palm facing her and shake my head.

"I need some time alone." I say and she looks sad, but nods her head in agreement.

CHAPTER SEVEN

Stranger in the Forest

I walk blindly through the forest. I'm looking without actually seeing anything. My mind is reeling with this revelation, and I'm a prisoner in my own thoughts.

I only thought I wanted answers.

Somewhere in the distance the rushing, bubbling sound of running water drifts to my ears and it acts like a siren call. I have always loved rivers and streams.

Water that never stands still creates a reverent and respectful calm in me. I think I relate because I hate the feeling of being stagnant and admire anything and anyone that can change constantly, always moving forward. Lately I seem to be stuck in the rut that is my life and it's distressing.

The sound pulls me up out of my troubled thoughts and draws me to it. I walk toward the sound, searching for the source. I tie my key back on my cord and put it back on my neck, dropping it down my shirt out of sight again along the way.

Standing on the crest of a small hill, I spot a small river. The trees around it are lush and green and the mossy rocks on the banks look inviting.

This looks like a good spot to think.

I sit down on a rock and take off my shoes and socks and set them on the bank behind me. I swing my feet into the icy river, which is shocking at first as I expect it to be, but the rush of the water through my toes and over my ankles feels relaxing despite being frigid. The water is crystal clear and I can see little fish darting around under the surface swerving through the current, sometimes going with and other times against it. It looks like they're participating in a playful dance with the water.

Soon the sounds of gurgling water and little birds in the trees set me at ease and my mood reroutes like the water running at my feet. I start to feel a sense of possibility instead of negativity.

'Right wrongs that are in our future, as well as our past . . .' I wonder what the savior is supposed to fix? If it really is me, how am I going to do this? I have so much to learn and still so many questions.

A movement reflected on the surface of the water right in front of me breaks through my distraction. The ripples don't let me see what it is right away, but I can see that it's big.

I slowly look up and a giant creature is standing there on the opposite bank of the river just looking at me. It looks vaguely familiar and is much, much bigger than I am. My hands start to tremble and fidget nervously.

I really *wish I had paid attention in our mythology units in literature class . . .*

It seems to be regarding me, sizing me up, just as I am doing the same. It has the face, arms and chest of a man, but it's body is the body of a horse. It's arms and torso are extremely muscular and sinewy. I take a moment despite my fear, to admire his build. A human man built like this would make me do a double take.

It's stomping one hoof, which draws my attention to his equally powerful looking legs.

Isn't that a sign of anger or displeasure in a horse? Oh crap. I'm in trouble. This thing is about to stomp me into a million pieces.

The name of what he is suddenly comes back to me.

A Centaur! Okay Dana, no sudden movements. Don't give this thing any reason to get spooked.

It speaks in a great, booming voice, but I can't understand it. The language it's speaking sounds a little like . . . Latin? It's hard to tell what it's intentions are.

Why didn't I just let Aurelia come with me. She would know what to do.

I cast my eyes down not wanting to seem challenging and I answer it as quietly as my voice allows me to. "I'm so sorry, I can't understand what you're saying."

But a thought strikes me: *Sing, Dana.*

So I start singing one of the more complicated, powerful songs I've learned, quiet and low. I don't want to startle him, but I want to try to make him understand that I am friendly in the only language I know of this place.

His reaction is startling. He immediately stops stomping. A look of recognition passes through the features of his face and he bows, then kneels down.

My breath catches in my throat and my song falters, but I recover it and finish. He continues to kneel.

"Sage, I apologize if I have startled you." he says in English!

"I . . . I'm sorry, I don't know what to say." I'm still nervous. "Why did you call me Sage?"

"The Great Prophecy of my people tells of the coming of the Sage. You are she, are you not?"

"How can you know that? My faerie isn't with me right now. Isn't that how you're told you'll recognize me?"

"Yes, but there are other ways. It is said that you were born from the spirit of a goddess. Her essence flows through you, endowing you with a beauty unlike any other. I can see it radiating from you like light," he pauses, "But strange," he muses wearing a puzzled look, "I also sense darkness in you . . . "

My cheeks flush hot despite my very cold feet.

"Please call me Dana." I stand and return his bow. "What should I call you?"

"My name is Cynbel."

"Well Cynbel, it's a pleasure to meet you." I try to speak with the same formality that he is using.

"Likewise, Sage," he splashes through the river to come to my side and kneels directly in front of me, bowing his head once again. "Climb up on my back and I'll take you back to your faerie. It's not safe for you so deep in the forest right now, especially without your guide."

Something tells me it would be impolite as well as unwise to refuse his offer, so I swoop up my shoes and scramble up on his huge back.

"Thank you, Cynbel."

"Think nothing of it, Sage."

I have never ridden a horse before, and find myself wondering if it is anything like this or if riding a Centaur is entirely different. I marvel at the feeling of every muscle in his body rippling beneath me. This is a majestic, beautiful being.

We arrive back at Séamus's cottage after a short run

for Cynbel and Aurelia is vigilantly waiting for me outside. As the huge Centaur kneels to allow me to slide to the ground easily, Aurelia flies up to me, hovering nervously. She is acting peculiarly.

Before he has a chance to stand up again, I kiss Cynbel softly on the cheek.

"Thank you again." I say.

This time he blushes and barely mumbles a reply saying something about 'his duty.'

He turns and thunders off through the trees, his powerful hooves beating a rhythm like tribal drums.

"Where did he come from?" Aurelia asks.

"I met him by the river. He scared me at first, but he knew who I was! Or . . . what I am or . . . something." I'm feeling confused about how to think of myself.

"How's Séamus? Can he talk? There are still so many things left unanswered, and now I have a few new questions."

"He's okay, I think. He's been drinking water and ate little. His strength seems to be returning some." Aurelia is somber.

I push through the heavy front door of Séamus's house and see him sitting up on the fur rug, propped against a chest. He does look stronger, moving more freely. I walk further into the room and sit on a rough hewn bench just across the fur rug from the chest, so that I am facing him. Aurelia flies over and nestles into my neck in the dip behind my collar bone, settling in under my hair. Soon she is breathing evenly, snoozing comfortably while I talk with our friend.

"Séamus, I'm sorry about earlier. I'm just so confused. I'm a human. Things like this just don't happen in our world. It's really hard to swallow."

"I know," Séamus says with a crooked smile.

"I still have a million questions," I say.

"Yes, yes, I know that too."

"So . . . what is a Templar? And why do they want to kill me?"

He takes a deep breath seeming to ready his weak body for a long explanation. "Well, the Templars were a religious group of people that got started in the 12th century. Their purpose was ta protect the interests of the Catholic Church. They were the Knights Templar, but they only lasted for a couple a hundred years. The Church dissolved them in the 14th century."

"How can there be a Templar following me around now if they haven't existed for hundreds of years? And why does he want to hurt me?"

"Dana." Séamus looks pensive, like he's holding something back and I don't make any qualms about letting the confusion show on my face. I don't need to act here. "The Great Prophecy is complicated . . . it says that yer purpose is to protect the Earth Mother. The exact way yer supposed to do that has not been revealed, but it's been said that the Catholic Church feels threatened by the Sage. I believe that the Templar that's after you is travelin' through time somehow. The Church has sent him after you in yer time ta keep you from rightin' any of the wrongs the Prophecy tells about."

"Why is the Church worried about the Prophecy? And what is a Sage? You haven't called me that before and now you're the second person to call me that within the hour."

"Nobody knows why the Church concerns itself with the details of the Prophecy, but the Sage is who the Prophecy refers to. It's you. It refers ta someone that's wise. Yer a talented Bard at the tender age of 18 with virtually no trainin' at all. It's unheard of, Dana. It takes years and years of trainin' to produce a Bard that can do the things you can do already."

My mind begins to try to connect the dots.

So much information! I suppose I have always been pretty different from other people my own age. I've always thought I could feel things and sense things other people didn't seem to notice . . .

"Wait, who else called you Sage?"

"It was Cynbel. The centaur in the forrest. I met him at the river and he gave me a ride back here." Séamus's eyes widen and his mouth drops open.

"You met a centaur in the forest?" he asks excitedly.

"Yeah, why?"

"The centaurs don't show themselves ta people and they're fierce creatures! They'd just as soon kill you, than talk ta you. But . . . he definitely called you Sage? And he gave you a ride, you say?"

I nod my head, slightly speechless.

"Huh. He recognized you," he says very matter-of-factly. He sounds a little relieved and somewhat pleased with himself as if this is a confirmation somehow that he is right about me. "What did he say ta you? How did he know who you are?"

"I asked him the same thing! The text talks about my faerie, but Aurelia wasn't with me. He said he could see the light of the essence of my goddess spirit shining through me?" I shrug. "What did he mean by that?"

"Hmm," he pauses, "I have no idea."

He also said that he can see darkness in me. Is that going to be a problem?

My dream comes flooding back to me. "Séamus," I begin quietly. "There's one more thing I need to ask about then I'll let you get some rest."

"Of course, Dana. Ask whatever you need ta."

"I had a dream, only . . . I don't think it was a dream. I felt the way I did the first few times I came to the Otherworld. I was conscious of my surroundings, I could think, smell and feel . . ." I tell the story of the dream while Séamus listens intently.

". . . the same Templar from New York actually stabbed me in my 'dream', but he was wearing different clothes . . . Then he was wearing the same clothes . . . It was a weird dream that was hard to follow. "

Séamus looks deeply troubled. "I think what you might have seen was a vision of a possible future. Visions are not prophetic. Nothin' is set in stone, so I don't think you need ta worry. You can change the future at any time, but I think we should consult Merlin 'bout this one just ta be sure. When you come back ta stay we can make the journey. I'm afraid I need ta rest up first."

"Okay, Séamus. You rest and I'm going to get your place back in order." I put Aurelia on the fur with Séamus so she can sleep too. She's had a long day as well.

Séamus nods and turns over, closing his eyes and I spend the evening cleaning.

I put the cottage back together, singing while I turn the furniture back up the way it belongs and sweep up the shards of the broken dishes and pottery. I mop up the blood and before long the cottage looks like nothing has happened.

I stand back, smiling at my handiwork and notice that it's gotten late and I'm feeling tired too, so I look around for a place to sleep. I really haven't been in any other area of the cottage than the main room, so I go exploring. I peek in doors that I've never opened and find a couple of bedrooms. One of them is obviously Séamus's room because it looks used. The bed linens are turned back and disheveled. And there are a couple of items of clothing thrown over the footboard of the bed.

His mom must not have made him make his bed.

A second bedroom is made up perfectly and everything is in order.

No one must be using this one. I'll just slip into bed and I'll put it all back the way I found it tomorrow.

I crawl in under the covers and the mattress is filled with goose down. It feels like laying on a cloud! It's so warm and comfortable and I am so worn out from such a long, weird day that my eyes close instantly. It feels like moments later they open to daylight and the smells of something delicious cooking.

Where is that heavenly smell coming from?

I rub my eyes trying to clear away the grogginess, swing my feet over the edge of the bed, and stand up. For a moment I forget where I am. I look around me, slightly confused by my surroundings and then it dawns on me.

Right. I'm in Séamus's extra bedroom. I can hear someone up and about in the main room of the cottage.

Who could that be?

I quickly make the bed and pad out into the main room. Aurelia is scampering along the countertop helping with preparations while Séamus cooks over the hearth.

"Séamus! What are you doing? Shouldn't you be resting?"

"Yer awake!"

"Yeah, I am, but I don't think you should be!" I say.

"Oh, now. I'm feelin' much better. I made you some breakfast," he says, smiling at me proudly, slightly hunched over in front of the cook fire. I can tell that his wounds are bothering him more than he's letting on.

I reach to pull back the sleeve of his left arm that he's holding stationary across his belly as if it were in a sling, and he swats my hand with his wooden spoon!

"Séamus!" I scold. "I'm only trying to take a look at the cut on your arm. Let me see it, please."

He looks down defeatedly and holds out his arm to me slowly, wincing when he moves it and I pull back his sleeve tenderly. He has changed the rag that I wrapped around his arm to help stop the bleeding, but I can see that there's still blood seeping from the wound. It is beginning to soak the rag again, though it's not quite as blood-stained as it was last night.

I gently pull the rag back and the cut is gaping.

That definitely needs stitches . . .

I haven't seen many cuts that need stitches in my life, but common sense tells me that this cut is too deep to heal without some help.

"We're going to have to figure out something to do for you today. Your cuts can't stay like this. They'll take too long to heal and you'll get an infection. I'm guessing we won't just be able to get you some antibiotics at the local drug store."

"I don't know what yer goin' ta be able ta do for me . . . " he trails off as he realizes he must relent and allow me to help him.

An idea hits me in the face and a lightbulb must have gone off over my head.

"What is it, Dana?" Aurelia asks.

"Well, why can't I just draw Séamus whole again, like I

did for you?"

Séamus shakes his head. "Ya can't do that. It worked for Aurelia because she's yer creation. Yer like her God. Understand?"

I'm visibly disappointed, but I nod my head silently.

I suppose that would have been too easy.

"I'm going to go back into the forest to see if Cynbel has any ideas then," I say.

"That's fine, but you have ta eat yer breakfast first!"

I smile at him suppressing a giggle. It feels like I have yet another parent.

And just when I am supposed to be leaving the nest, but guess I shouldn't resent being cared for. There are a lot of people who aren't lucky enough to have one person that cares for them, much less as many as I have.

I finish my breakfast of a bowl of sweet, oatmeal-like porridge.

"Thank you for breakfast, Séamus. I'm off to see what I can find out. Is there anything I can do for you before I go?" I ask hugging him lightly and taking my bowl to the sink, just like at home. While there's no range-top for cooking, he does have running water, thank goodness.

"No, I can get around. I'll just try ta relax here as much as I can and do some readin'. I think I'll read about yer trainin'!" He says, obviously feeling pretty good about his idea.

I smile at him and head for the door with Aurelia trailing after me.

CHAPTER EIGHT

Bébinn of Fourknocks

Once outside I glance around nervously, sensing a difference in the forest. I have been feeling apprehensive that the Templar has paid an unwelcome visit to the Otherworld, and my nerves have been on end since we found Séamus unconscious and bleeding yesterday morning. I'm gripped by hyper-awareness, wondering if and when he will return, but *this* presence doesn't feel menacing . . . only present.

"Aurelia come close," I hiss.

Better safe than sorry.

"Is something wrong?" she asks, zipping up to my shoulder, to assume her place of protection.

"I'm not sure, but something is different . . ." I tell her in a low whisper. I put my finger to my lips. "Shh, let me listen."

I stand at the edge of Séamus's little cottage yard listening to the sounds of the forest. I can hear birds, some crows, but not hundreds of them like yesterday, just normal, happy birdsongs. There are squirrels chattering at each other in the treetops. A breeze blows softly through the leaves in the canopy. All seems well, but then I hear a twig snap close by.

"Is someone there?" I call out loudly.

A large figure emerges from the dark edge of the forrest into the light in the cottage's small clearing.

I release the breath I had been involuntarily holding. It's only Cynbel.

"Wow! You had me pretty nervous!" I tell him.

"Sage, there is no need for you to be nervous. You are well protected here in Tir na nÓg," he says motioning with his hand in a short movement, elbow bent, hand in the air, as if waving someone forward.

I stand in awe as one by one, approximately 20 centaurs emerge from their strategic locations in the edges of the forest, completely surrounding Séamus's house.

Cynbel gestures to a beautiful female Centaur to his right.

"This is Epona, my mate," she bows low as he finishes up his introduction.

"It's a pleasure to meet you, Epona. My name is Dana," I say bowing in her direction as well, "and this is Aurelia." She closes her eyes and nods her head to me gracefully.

My God, these creatures are so impressive! Just gorgeous!

A slight blush colors Epona's cheeks and my brows furrow.

What in the . . . ?

Cynbel's deep voice brings me back from my thoughts. "Epona, myself, and these 25 centaurs that make up our tribe are here to serve and protect you, Sage. We offer you our services for whatever you may need. I saw in your thoughts yesterday that some misfortune had befallen your friend and teacher in the cottage and we've been keeping watch here since."

Well that answers that. They can read my thoughts . . .

Epona laughs heartily. "Yes, Sage. That is one of our many talents. We're also fierce warriors and we've all vowed to protect you on the long journey ahead," she says with her arm extending out to her side, palm facing forward she gestures to the circle of giants around me.

My cheeks feel hot. This could be quite an advantage, but also a bit embarrassing. I shake it off remembering that I was looking for them today anyway.

How lucky for me that they were right outside!

"How can we help you?" Epona asks in her silky voice. She speaks with a grace that matches her movements.

"My friend Cynbel mentioned is in need of help. He has been badly injured by an enemy whose attack I narrowly escaped, thanks to my tiny friend here." I say with a slow sideways nod in Aurelia's direction. She lights up with pride like a nightlight.

"A Templar?" Cynbel asks.

I nod once in reply. I sense that extra words and motions are not necessary with these majestic people. They read as much in my movements and thoughts as I do in most others around me. It's nice to be able to use more subtle forms of communication with them. Sometimes conversations with other humans can be so tedious.

"My friend, whose name is Séamus, has some very deep wounds that need caring for, but I have no resources here. I could go back to my home in the human world to get some things that would help him, but I hesitate to leave him in the state he's in and I might not necessarily have access to the supplies that are available in the human world either."

Epona nods, kneeling down, gesturing for me to climb up on her back as I did yesterday with Cynbel.

"We know someone that may be able to help you. She is a scholar here in Tir na nÓg. Bébinn lives in the village of Fourknocks."

"Tir na nÓg?" I ask.

"It's where we are," she says matter-of-factly.

Must be what they call the Otherworld.

"Yes, that is correct, Sage."

I exhale a sigh, feeling slightly frustrated that every thought I have is subject to the centaurs' scrutiny.

"Please call me Dana," I say a little more irritably than I intend.

"As you wish."

Only Epona and Cynbel accompany Aurelia and me on the trip to Fourknocks. The two Centaurs assure me the trip is a short one on four hooves, that we'll be back by evening.

The remaining tribesmen stay behind to maintain the perimeter they've established around Séamus's house, ensuring he'll be well guarded if the Templar returns to the scene of the crime.

On Epona's back I sit as far forward as I can, so I can wrap my arms around her waist. It's shocking to feel that she is just as muscular as her male counterpart.

What amazing creatures these centaurs are!

Cynbel laughs aloud and I glance sidelong in his direction. I see him looking at me with something like pride glowing in his eyes and I laugh along, resigning myself to the idea that no thought I will have in the presence of these creatures will be private.

Oh well . . . I suppose it isn't a horrible thing for them to be able to read admiration and respect in my thoughts.

I set my gaze firmly forward, scanning the forest for anything out of the ordinary and the centaurs thunder toward our destination, quickly merging onto a primitive forest road that appears rarely traveled. We continue on it for the better part of the morning only stopping when the sun is high overhead to drink from a river running next to the road.

"We need to stop and rest for a few moments," Cynbel says as he wades into the water. Epona kneels so that I might slide off her back and I am grateful for the break. My pelvic bones have caused quite the bruises to develop in my nether regions.

Who would have thought riding horseback would be so hard on your body!

I stand and stretch for a few minutes trying not to dwell on how sore my rear-end feels, but the discomfort is making me walk funny and I've still got a long ride ahead.

I'm going to have to talk to them about getting a saddle or something in Fourknocks. This is ridiculous.

I wade into the water and lower my cupped hands into the river. The water is clean, pure and cold. It feels good going down.

Epona approaches me. "Dana, we can get you a padded blanket to throw over my back when we get to our destination if you want. You aren't the first human to feel discomfort after a long ride on the back of a centaur.

I feel a bit embarrassed, but I look at her with what I hope looks like gratitude and not misery, nodding my head.

"Thanks, Epona."

"We have arrived, by the way," Cynbel announces.

"The village of Fourknocks is just over the hill there."

He points to a small rise in the road just ahead.

"Mind if I walk along side you for the remainder of the trip?" I ask not wanting to get on Epona's back again right now. My pelvis needs a rest.

"You may walk between us, Sage," Cynbel says. I do as he says and as we crest the top of the hill a beautiful cobblestone road unfolds before us. About a mile or so ahead I can see a quaint little town with red tiled roofs and a building larger than all the rest in the center. There is activity at every entrance to the wall.

How lovely!

Our group saunters along the road, the two centaurs standing guard on each side with me sandwiched in between them. Aurelia perches on my shoulder facing the way we came to keep watch behind us as instructed by Cynbel.

They really take this protecting me thing seriously.

I can just imagine how ridiculous we must look. I crane my neck to get a view of the approaching countryside, but I can't see much over the backs of these giant creatures. Standing only 5'5" tall, I am dwarfed in comparison to the pair.

We draw near to the gate and I can see out in front of us. It looks like the small town holds quite a population. The hustle and bustle within looks exciting!

Cynbel's deep voice interrupts my musings, leaning down to talk in a low voice in my ear.

"Sage, it is necessary to stay in this formation while inside the city walls. There are so many people inside that it would be easy for someone to get to you unless you walk between us. I don't think anyone would be stupid enough to try to snatch you from between two centaurs, but if anyone tries they'll soon see why they shouldn't have.

I want you to rest your arm on Epona's shoulder and walk exactly even with it. I'm going to stagger back slightly. I don't want it to be so obvious that we're guarding you. No need to draw attention."

Not long into our walk into the town it becomes obvious that I am drawing attention regardless of our formation.

Must be my clothes and my hair.

The general population is wearing simple peasant clothing. Most of the women wear dresses without decoration and men wear pants and tunics made of fabrics in subdued colors. My jeans, and my t-shirt and hoodie with florescent colored accents certainly set me apart from the crowd, but I don't mind. The prophecy did say that I wouldn't be dressed like the people of this world.

We make our way down the main thoroughfare, turning right onto another large, but winding street that takes us away from the rows of shop-type buildings to an area with a more residential feel. Along the way the streets are filled with people leading donkeys pulling carts, people carrying baskets of goods, lean-to shacks with vendors inside selling wares, and people with their heads down, rushing to unknown destinations. All of them give me a once over with curious looks on their faces with the exception of those in a hurry. They seem distracted by whatever mission they're on and don't seem to be aware of their surroundings at all. There are other Centaurs milling around that give Cynbel and Epona silent nods as we pass, and a myriad of other strange creatures that I have never seen before, and have no idea what they are.

"Isn't this place incredible?" Aurelia squeaks excitedly in my ear.

"Yeah, it's definitely a great place to people-watch . . . and creature watch! I just wish we had some time to explore. We'll have to come back here when we have more time to stay," I reply.

We arrive at a rather large structure on the outskirts of town. Upon first glance I notice that the building has several floors, primitive looking stained-glass windows, and a huge arched doorway with a heavy door made of large timbers. It hangs on wrought iron hinges, sports a twisted wrought iron handle, and a heavy wrought iron door-knocker.

Epona lifts the ring of the knocker and brings it down hard on it's knocker plate a couple of times, then we wait expectantly.

The door opens slowly and a beautiful woman stands in the doorway with a questioning look on her face. Her frame is slight and she appears to be about my height. She wears a long shift dress adorned with tiny embroidery accents around the collar, the sleeve cuffs, and hem. Her wavy hair is jet black and hangs loosely to her hips. Her eyes twinkle kindly and she smiles at our group.

"Greetings friends," recognition shows in her expression as she greets the centaurs, but when her gaze falls on me, there is a momentary hitch in her greeting. Her breath catches, her voice trails off, and her face takes on a blank look all in an instant. She recovers quickly, smiling again.

"Sage," she says quietly, first glancing around us into the street in all directions as if to be sure no one could hear her say it, then bowing her head in my direction. "Come in, come in."

She glides backward out of the doorway to allow us room to enter her home, which as far as I could tell is one of the only buildings in town large enough to accommodate the centaurs.

The lady closes the door behind us and turns back to our group. She reaches out and takes my hand in both of hers and kneels gracefully in front of me, pressing her forehead to the top of my hand.

"It is an honor to have you here," she says, holding her position.

"Please," I begin nervously, unsure what to think of her display, "My name is Dana. Please call me Dana."

What is wrong with these people?

She rises and looks me directly in the eyes. Her eyes hold mine hostage, as if by magical force. My heart flutters and I feel an unexplainable physical connection with this woman. I am unable to look away and the room around me blurs, going completely silent. I am suddenly drifting in a haze where only the two of us are present.

"I am Bébinn of Fourknocks," her voice is made of mesmerizing bells. "I know who you are and why you're here."

The idea that her lips are not moving registers in my mind, but doesn't alarm or shock me in any way. Something deep inside me blooms like a flower and an awareness opens with it filling me with warmth and love. The feeling is absolutely invigorating as it overtakes and displaces every particle of self-loathing I have been carrying with me these past months.

"Do you know who you are, my Sage?" Bébinn

continues our mental conversation smiling dreamily and then I know that I am Dana, but I am also someone else. I see images of us as little girls in her mind. We are running in a field, hand in hand, but she is not she and I am not me. We are both someone else.

Knowledge of a different time spills forth from the flower of awareness. "Yes," I answer her. "I am Morrígan."

A tear slips out of her eye, sliding silently down her cheek and our thoughts intertwine, dancing together. "And I am Éire . . . your,"

"Sister," we say together.

"I have searched for you for thousands of years, sister." She releases her mental hold, but our physical connection continues unchanged. There is an energy flowing between us that I know cannot be broken now. She kisses my left cheek, lingering there, then my right and embraces me in a tight hug. I hug her back with all my might.

Regardless of the physical impossibility in the human world that this woman is my sister, I know that what I saw and heard in her mind is true. It is a certainty that I feel over reason and possibility.

The room comes back into focus and the two centaurs are watching us curiously, but the looks on their faces make me believe that they could not hear our internal dialogue.

Aurelia seems to be the most perplexed of our group and shoots me a look that says: *what the heck was that?*

I only shrug at her slightly. I wouldn't know how to explain what just happened even if I wanted to.

"It is my great pleasure to welcome the four of you to Fourknocks. How may I be of assistance to you today?"

Bébinn speaks aloud.

"We must keep up the appearance that we do not know each other for now," she says inside my mind again. *"At least until we have some time so I can tell the story the way it should be told."*

"Okay, I'll play along." It's so hard to suppress the childish grin that threatens to break out on my face as I realize I can "talk" to her in the same way.

"I have a friend who lives in the forest who has been badly injured. Cynbel suggested that you might be able to help us. My friend's wounds are very deep and need to be stitched up as we would do in the human world, but without human medicine I'm afraid it would be too painful."

Bébinn looks thoughtful for a moment. "I believe I may have a Physik book or three in my collection," she says looking around the inside of the building.

I follow her gaze and I gasp loudly. My initial encounter with Bébinn was so all-encompassing that I somehow failed to notice that the walls of this beautiful building are lined with books!

She starts walking toward one end of the room and I follow her.

"What is this place?" I ask in awe.

"This is my family's private collection of books. The way you are a Bard, I am a Druid: a keeper of knowledge here in Tir na nÓg." She runs her fingers along the spines of her beautiful treasures. Stopping on one, she quickly taps it.

"This one has what you need, sister." I hear inside my head.

Bébinn runs the tip of her finger to the top of the book's spine and hooks it in the top edge, tipping the book out carefully into her hand. She walks to a pedestal and sets the book down on top of it tenderly.

"Our ancestors did not believe in writing our stories down or keeping written records of anything. We didn't even have a written language. Because of this, the Bard Order was entrusted to preserve the histories and stories of our people orally. When Christianity took hold in Ireland however, the Druids were forced to hide their beliefs. This made it too hard to teach new generations of Bards the historic songs. It was dangerous to sing them aloud and our history began to be lost to us."

She turns pages as she talks.

"One grandfather, far back in my family line, learned to write and began to write the stories down. As bookbinding and printing became common, he began collecting books. He and his sons secreted many books away, successfully hiding them here during periods of book burning in the Human World. My family has always been able to travel easily between the Otherworld and the Human World." She winks at me and I smile knowing that her family is somehow also my family.

"I found it!" she exclaims. "You said he needed to be stitched up, yes?"

I nod.

"You're going to need a few herbs to help you do this. It says here that Valerian root will induce a deep sleep, Hypericum will help with pain control, and Yarrow will help cleanse the wounds and arrest bleeding. We'll make a tea with the first two and muddle the Yarrow in water with a mortar and pestle and apply that to his wounds topically."

Cynbel and Epona overhear the good news.

"You have the knowledge you seek, Sage?" he asks loudly, his voice echoing around the large room.

"Yes, but I am going to need to get the herbs we need

before we return to Séamus."

"I can help you get those here in Fourknocks," Bébinn says. "Then, if it's okay with Cynbel and Epona, I would like to accompany you back to your friend to be of assistance."

"I will never leave your side again, my Morrígan." Bébinn's voice echoes inside my head and I can feel her devotion to me. I don't care what I have to do to make it happen, but I won't let her leave my side again either.

Epona speaks up. "One of us can certainly carry Bébinn. It is not a problem."

"Thank you, Epona." I say gratefully.

Aurelia flies up to my face squeaking excitedly. "Can I kiss Bébinn with understanding, so she can talk to me too?"

"Of course, you can!" I say. "Will it work? I thought you could only do that for me?"

She winks at me. "Definitely! You're the same," she says cryptically.

Aurelia quickly flies to Bébinn hovering in front of her face gesturing wildly at her cheek. Somehow it seems that Bébinn knows what Aurelia wants to do and she holds her cheek forward, allowing Aury to 'hug' and kiss her.

Bébinn holds a hand to the cheek where she received the kiss and smiles broadly. "Amazing!" she exclaims.

I'm not sure, but I'm guessing, based on Bébinn's reaction, even in the Otherworld it's not every day that one is kissed by a faerie. I laugh out loud when Epona confirms my thought.

"No, a faerie kiss is very special, indeed, Dana!" The female centaur chuckles, dropping a bit of the formality characteristic of the speech of their race.

CHAPTER NINE

Sisters Unite

Bébinn gathers some of her personal effects and throws them in a leather satchel, similar to a messenger bag. As we exit her personal library, she closes the giant door and leaves her hand on the handle briefly. I can see the exchange of energy between her body and the door. Unlike the sparks that flew when Séamus tried to touch my key, it's subtle and positive, unhindered.

She pushes on the door to test its resistance and when she's satisfied it won't budge our motley crew ambles out into the street. I am again walking between the two centaurs with Bébinn now walking out front leading the way.

"Where are we going to get Séamus's herbs?" I ask her.

"There is a merchant up ahead that will have everything we need," she says over her shoulder keeping her eyes ahead and vigilant.

Our walk is short this time and soon we're standing in front of a shop that could exist in the Human World. It has a glass front display window set up with beautiful, old fashioned merchandise displays just inside them.

"We'll keep watch in the street," Cynbel says as the centaurs take a spot on each side of the door reminding me of sentinels. "We're a bit too big for this building."

"Alright," Bébinn chimes.

When she, Aurelia and I walk into the shop a small bell rings above our heads alerting the shop attendant to our presence. Once inside the strong smells hit me in the face, but they're not unpleasant. Florals mingling with herbal smells mingling with spice smells create a symphony of aromas that my nose must quickly adjust to.

"Welcome . . ." the attendant notices me walking in behind Bébinn. ". . . Travelers." Her face belies her curiosity mixed with repulsion.

She obviously doesn't buy into the Prophecy . . . I grin to myself.

"How might I help you today?"

Bébinn speaks up. "We're looking for a few specific herbs. I was hoping you would have them all here. We need them quickly, so we can't take the time to gather them for ourselves. Do you have Valerian Root, Hypericum and Yarrow?"

"Oh yes," the shop owner says smiling. "Those are fairly common herbs. Follow me."

She turns and walks toward the back of the store, stopping at a cabinet that holds tools. She pulls a small burlap, drawstring bag and a knife from inside the cabinet and walks brusquely to a couple of dried herb bundles hanging on the wall. She cuts a handful of each from the hanging bundles, then reaches into a small basket pulling out a root. She stows all the herbs in the burlap bag.

"What can you offer in trade, Travelers?" she asks, still

looking somewhat put-off by my appearance.

I rifle around in my pockets feeling a little embarrassed and my fingers brush across a crinkly piece of paper. I pull out a dollar bill.

I've got money? How long has that been in there?

I extend the found dollar to her and she takes it turning it over and feeling it skeptically.

"What is this? A piece of paper?"

"I'm sorry," I say. "I don't have anything else."

Dammit, why didn't I bring my backpack? I've got all kinds of interesting things in there!

"Show her the key, Morrígan."

I throw Bébinn a questioning look, but she nods.

What the heck, why not?

I reach into my t-shirt collar and pull the key out by its cord, lifting it over my head. When I set it down on her counter and push it forward, I glance at the shopkeeper and see a look of mild curiosity spreading across her features.

"I love this part!" Aurelia squeaks jumping up and down on my shoulder, clapping her hands.

I watch her little excited dance making a great effort not to laugh along. I don't think laughing would help my plight any.

The attendant bends over the counter and slowly reaches to touch the key, but it slides away from her hand, just as it did for Séamus. Her eyes widen in surprise and her head jerks up. Recognition registers suddenly and she stands up straight, closes her eyes, and bows her head.

"Forgive me, Sage. I did not know who you were. You're welcome, of course, to anything I have here. They are gifts, no trade needed."

As I pick up the key she slides my dollar back to me as well.

"No, please keep it. If anyone from the Human World ever comes in to your shop and they see that, they'll know you're friendly." I chuckle.

How likely is it someone from the Human World will ever step foot in here again? Not *likely, but whatever. She gives me gifts, I give her a gift.*

I take the burlap bag and Bébinn, Aurelia and I turn toward the door to leave. "Safe travels, Sage," the shopkeeper calls after us.

Outside Cynbel and Epona are waiting, both with padded horse blankets on their backs.

"Epona! Thank you!" I exclaim. "You remembered!"

"Yes, Dana. I got them for you while you were in the herb shop," she smiles.

When she kneels, I kiss her cheek and hug her before clambering up onto her back.

Once in position and now a bit more comfortable than I was on the ride into town, I take stock of our surroundings and notice that the shadows have grown long, and just in front of me on the top of a building are three crows.

Crows again . . . that's odd, I've been seeing them everywhere lately.

"I think we need to get a move on. It's getting late," I say slightly unnerved by their watchful stare.

Dana, you're being ridiculous. It's only a few crows.

"Yes, Sage. You're right," Cynbel chimes in. "We will not be stopping on the way back to Séamus's house. You'll need to hold on tight once we go through the gate."

I nod in agreement.

The centaurs settle into a light trot on a different road through the village than we   traveled coming in. The crowds of people have thinned a little as well, making it possible to move through the town faster than before. As we approach what must be a side entrance to Fourknocks we slow to navigate the throng of people entering and exiting and I see him.

The Templar is standing in a dark doorway. He is dressed in the same manner he was in New York and is watching us like a hawk, just as he did at the Met.

I gasp as a pang of recognition comes from the flower of awareness in a sudden rush that takes my breath. *How could I possibly know this nut job?* I brush off the feeling.

"Éire, there in the doorway. The Templar is here."

I see Bébinn turn her gaze in the direction of mine, slowly, undetectably. She leans forward into Cynbel's back and whispers to him.

"Hold on," he says in my direction and I lace my fingers together around Epona's waist just in time to keep myself from falling backward as the two centaurs take a great leap over the heads of the remaining people in front of us, narrowly missing a few when they land on the road outside the gate.

Ugh, that really hurt.

They keep right on running without missing a beat. The wind howls through my hair and my heart pounds a drumbeat in my chest to match the beating hooves of the two centaurs. I glance back and see that the Templar is not pursuing us, but strangely there are now five crows flying behind us, keeping up with our pace.

"Éire, what's with the crows? I am beginning to see them all the time."

"They're a part of you, Morrígan. You'll soon understand, my

sister."

I shake off the fear that grips me and turn my attention to the task of staying on my centaur's back while she runs at breakneck speed. The blanket is helping my sore rear, but at this rate of speed it's slipping around underneath me forcing me to work twice as hard to stay seated on Epona's back.

Thankfully the trip is much shorter at this pace and we arrive at Séamus's house quickly. Our escorts greet the tribe and talk about the trip. Cynbel tells them that we saw the Templar and together they discuss his continued presence in Tir na nÓg, assessing the potential risk he poses while I dismount and take our burlap bag full of goodies inside with Bébinn and Aurelia.

I open the cottage door and walk in first, finding Séamus lounging on the furry rug with his books and some water.

"Séamus, how are you feeling?" I ask timidly. I'm regretting what I am about to have to do. My stomach isn't really squeamish, but it also isn't made of steel. Blood doesn't bother me, but I can't imagine myself sewing up someone's wounds.

Too bad I'm about to. My stomach lurches.

"I'm alright. Who've you brought back with you then?"

"Oh this is Bébinn of Fourknocks," I say smiling from Séamus to her. "Will it be alright if she stays with us tonight? She is the scholar that helped us find some information to help you out."

"Of course it's alright! Make yerself at home, Bébinn! And thank you for yer help," he winks at her and Bébinn laughs heartily.

"Thank you, Séamus. Now, should we get started on

you?"

He looks a little alarmed. "It's goin' ta hurt, isn't it?" he asks.

"It may a tiny bit, but we brought some things to help with that," I reassure him.

I open the burlap bag and spill its contents onto the counter where we normally prepare the food. Aurelia settles on Séamus's shoulder patting his cheek and 'hugging' him.

"If her efforts don't help him, nothing will. Poor thing." I say to Bébinn mentally. She cuts her eyes at me giggling as quietly as she can.

"Oh! I almost forgot," I say scurrying out the front door. Outside the centaurs are still strategizing and I approach Epona quietly so I don't interrupt. At a break in the conversation she turns to me and smiles.

"What is it, Dana?"

"Well, I need to sew up Séamus's wounds, but to do that I need a strong thread that will resist breaking. I was wondering if I might cut a few hairs from your tail, Epona? Horse hair is the best thing for the job I can think of here in the Otherworld."

"Of course. I am happy to help," she replies handing me her knife.

What a trusting soul.

She shoots me a look that says, *I am, but you'd better be careful,* and I chuckle to myself as I cut three long hairs and pull on each end to test their strength.

Yep, these will do fine.

"Thank you," I say leaning my head on her side and stroking her back.

I went from no friends at all to five great ones almost all at once. I'm beginning to really love these creatures.

She looks back at me briefly with an awkward half-smile just before I run back inside.

In the cottage I hang a big pot of water and a metal teapot over the cook fire to get them boiling then turn my attention to Séamus.

"Séamus, I just need one last thing: a needle." His face turns ashen and he points to a desk to the right of his book shelf. "First drawer," he says shakily.

When I find the needle I bend it slightly into a bow shape and throw it into the pot along with the horse hair to sterilize them.

"Bébinn, can you help me prepare the herbs? I'm guessing you'll know a bit more about this part than I do." She smiles and nods and we set to the task of grinding the Hypericum and Yarrow, and chopping the Valerian Root into tiny pieces. While we work we hum a few of the Bardic songs together to pass the time which makes Séamus smile despite his nervous state.

We make a tea with the Valeria Root and Hypericum, adding a little honey so it isn't so bitter.

"Séamus, drink this down, okay?" Bébinn offers him a cup of the tea and he takes it reluctantly.

Next I prepare the muddled Yarrow paste to promote healing, wash my hands, and it's time to get to the dirty work. He's trying hard to stay awake, but I see Séamus's head nod several times while I am working on the Yarrow paste.

Bébinn fishes the needle and horse hairs from the pot and comes to sit beside me. I heave a giant nervous sigh and look at Bébinn.

"What if I can't do this?"

"Oh Sister, you can do anything, you must remember this. I am here with you as I have been throughout the eons. I will help you

114

always."

"Thank you, Éire." She puts her forehead to mine. Our eyes close and I can feel the energy flowing between us renewing my self-confidence. I take a deep breath and set to work unwrapping the blood-soaked rags from Séamus's arms. Most of his injuries are concentrated on his forearms.

He must have shielded himself with his arms, but I still don't know how he managed to fend off his attacker. Why did the Templar leave without killing him if that was the goal?

Together, Bébinn and I flush Séamus's deep cuts with warm water and I carefully sew up each one, knotting every horse hair stitch as I go. The job is no easy task for my untrained hands and takes several hours. When I am finally finished, I'm covered in blood and exhausted. I collapse on Bébinn's shoulder, relieved to be finished and somewhat nauseated.

We slather Séamus's cuts with the Yarrow paste and wrap them in fresh, clean rags.

I address Aurelia who has been working her calming magic on Séamus through the whole, hours-long process. "Aurelia, thank you! You helped so much!" I give her an index finger 'kiss' and she must be just as tired as I am because she just looks at me dreamily through half closed eyelids, flashing me a big goofy grin, before settling on Séamus's shoulder and passing out.

I scoop her up and get her settled on my pillow in my room, and Bébinn helps me get Séamus to his own bedroom to sleep for the night.

After the two of us clean up all the preparation and reparation messes in the main room of the cottage I look down at myself and feel disgusting. I'm covered in blood from my endeavors. I really need a bath!

I can't go home like this tomorrow, but I'm so tired.

Bébinn disappears into the other part of the cottage and after a few moments I hear water running. I'm too tired to be curious and before long my eyes are closing right where I sit in front of the fire.

I wake half-heartedly to a hand on my arm as Bébinn is pulling me up, supporting my weight and leading me toward the back of the cottage. She takes me into the bathroom and holds me up while I get undressed, then guides me into a bathtub of steaming water.

"Oh the water feels so good. My bottom is so sore from the ride to Fourknocks and my arms are tired and sore from fixing Séamus up all night."

"It's okay, Morrígan, just relax."

Bébinn washes my hair while I get the rest of me cleaned and presentable. I try to talk to her a little while I bathe.

"So . . . can you tell me more about the crows . . . and who are Morrígan and Éire? How are we them, but we're us? I mean, I know we're sisters, but . . . how?"

"We'll talk it all through tomorrow, sister. For now, we need to get some rest," she says handing me a towel.

I step out and get dried off, then put my pajamas on and fall into my bed, careful to avoid Aurelia.

Bébinn lays down next to me, snuggles up to my back and I feel complete.

I go to sleep with a smile on my face.

In this life I have always been an only child, how wonderful it is to have a sister.

Despite feeling peaceful and happy as I drift off to sleep, through the night I dream of dark things. I see myself dressed in strange clothes, wearing thick leather guards in pieces over my whole body; it's some kind of armor.

In one hand I'm holding a shield and in the other a sword. I'm wearing a small dagger strapped to my right thigh. The key hangs around my neck, and my hair is braided, with jet black feathers woven into the braid, tied with leather cord. The crow on my shoulder wears the same leather cords around one leg.

In my dream I look like myself, but I think of myself as Morrígan, not Dana. I am training with the sword in some kind of arena with men all around me dressed in chainmail and combinations of leather armor like mine and metal armor.

There are crows everywhere. Éire is with me watching the training taking place. She cheers as I knock an opponent off his feet with my shield, but my glance at her laughing, breaks my concentration. I don't notice that my opponent has jumped up quickly and I'm left vulnerable to his parry.

His blow sends me flying through the air and my vision is black, but Éire's voice drifts to me in the darkness.

"Morrígan . . . Morrígan . . ."

My eyes open and Bébinn is standing over me. I'm in Séamus's spare bedroom, and it's light outside.

"Today is the day that you go home, is it not?"

"Yes . . ." I say sadly. I love my parents, but I don't want to leave this place and my new friends and family. I especially don't want to leave Bébinn, but I haven't been able to think of a way for her to go with me. I don't think my parents will understand me bringing home a stray friend to stay at our house.

"Well let's get the day started," she says beaming at me.

The worst part of going home today is that I'm not sure how I'm going to tell Bébinn that I don't think I can take her with me.

"Morrígan, Séamus tells me that you're coming to live in Tir na nÓg soon. Is that so?"

"Yes, I will be coming back to stay any day now. I just have to wait a little longer for my plans to fall into place in the Human World."

"Then we won't be apart long. I think while you go back and prepare to come live here, I will stay with Séamus to help him as he heals."

I narrow my eyes and cock my head to the side, looking at her playfully in mock anger.

"Éire, can you hear my thoughts like the centaurs can? Even when I'm not actively talking to you in here?"

She bursts into laughter and nods her head.

I feign shock and outrage at the intrusion. "You little snake!" I hit her with a pillow and she falls on the floor laughing even harder.

"I'm sorry, Sister. I can't help it!" she is breathless, quaking with laughter.

"Why can't I hear yours?" I bellow like a whining child.

"I'm not sure. It may happen later. You haven't been using magic very long, after all. In fact, there are many things you'll begin to be able to do as you grow into your magic," she says winking.

"Oh," I say disappointed. "I was hoping you could teach me."

She kisses my forehead and beckons for me to follow her into the kitchen which is smelling like Heaven already.

At the hearth Séamus is up cooking again, and I resist

the urge to scold him. I think he should still be resting.

But he's a big boy, I suppose.

"Dana! Thank you, thank you for all you did! I feel like you put me back together!" He dances a little jig to meet me as I walk into the room and hugs me.

"So you're feeling pretty good, I take it?" I laugh.

Séamus's mood has infected Aurelia who is zooming around the room flying in corkscrew patterns and loop-da-loops.

"Aury, you're just showing off!" I call to her, laughing and joining in Séamus's jig even though I don't know a step of it.

"I'm feelin' great! Bébinn made me a weak tea this mornin' from the Hypericum and it's taken the edge offa the last bit of the pain I was feelin'.

By the way, you did a fine job of fixin' me up!"

"Aww, thanks, Séamus."

We all sit down in the chairs spread around the main room of the cottage and eat together. Between bites Bébinn tells our story:

"Dana, you asked me about the crows yesterday and I'm going to tell you, but first I have to start at the beginning of our story. You felt who you really are when we met, just as I did, but the Prophecy as we know it today is only part of the big picture."

Séamus looks from Bébinn to me and back to Bébinn with a very confused look on his face, while Aurelia just looks smug, like she already knows what my sister is going to say. I look at Bébinn expectantly, hungry to know everything.

"Thousands of years ago a prophet told of a female warrior, a Sage among Druids, that would change the course of all worlds in existence. The Bards wrote songs and poems about this woman that were passed down throughout history, but the story was changed along the way and parts of the original story were lost. Everything about the key and the faerie guide are correct, but the original story told the woman's name.

The Sage was called the Morrígan."

Séamus's sharp intake of breath startles me and he stares at me wide-eyed. He knows something I don't know!

"Now, you know that the Knights Templar are determined to squash the Prophecy, but you don't know that they have been determined to do so since their inception. That was the sole reason they were formed. The Church activated them as a special team of knights to search out and destroy the Morrígan, to put an end to the Prophecy once and for all.

It soon became clear to the Templars that the Morrígan was not the only threat to their Church, though. She and her sister Éire were so close that their energies fed off each other, making them very, very powerful; they were a force to be reckoned with.

The Morrígan, the Goddess of War was a shape shifter, and often took the form of a crow, flying over great battles to oversee their progress and protect her warriors. Éire was the Mother Goddess of Ireland and together they fought many wars never losing even one.

The secretive nature of the Knights' organization however, made them a truly formidable foe. It soon became clear that they posed a genuine threat to the sisters.

The Goddess Brighid recognized that the Morrígan and Éire were in grave danger, but they were very important to the Earth Mother, Danu, so Brighid devised a plan to temporarily save them from the Templars until she could find a way to destroy the Knights once and for all, (which she did by planting the seed of distrust in the Church leadership, but that's another story). In an act of desperation she killed the sisters' bodies and sent their spirits to the Isles of the Dead to be reborn.

I, Érie, was born here in Tir na nÓg and you, my sister, the Morrígan, were born in the Human World, where Brighid felt you would *never* be found. She thought the Templars would never expect what she did and she was right. It took them about a hundred years to catch on and it would have been a perfect plan, had they not found a way to send their men through time.

I wasn't told where you had been sent in the Human World and I often visited there hoping I would be able to feel you, but it was like searching for a needle in a haystack. Without your energy near mine, my magic was not strong enough to find you.

As it turns out, yours was strong enough alone to find me." She ends this story with a warm smile for me and grasps my hand firmly, holding it tight.

I am speechless, as is Séamus. Aurelia is smiling, like she knew it all along.

I look down. "I . . . I don't even know what to say." I hold my breath for a moment, the start of a long pause so I can gather my thoughts.

What I am about to say, I can only share with my sister.

"My human body has been through something so evil and ugly that just a month ago I didn't believe I was good enough to be alive. If you had told me then that I was a Goddess reborn as a Sage Bard destined to save the world, I would have laughed in your face. Just two days ago, I couldn't even believe I was the Sage the

Prophecy speaks of. Only when I met you did all the puzzle pieces click into place, and now I know in my heart what you say is true."

Bébinn pulls me into her embrace and hugs me while I weep. I shed tears of joy that I've found her, tears of sadness still mourning my lost innocence, and tears of relief that I can now let it all go and move forward with my new friends and family and my newly discovered purpose.

Séamus watches this all with mouth agape. "Well, now I know why Merlin was so insistent that I keep a close watch on you . . . It's definitely time for you ta make the trip ta meet him. No doubt about it.

Ta think I've had a Goddess under m'roof all this time. And now I got two!" he mutters under his breath staring into the fire, shaking his head.

"Séamus, it's about time for me to head home. My mom will be expecting me soon, but Bébinn is going to stay here while I'm tying up loose ends in the Human World. I don't think it will be very long before I'm back, okay?"

"Alright, young one . . . perhaps I should call ya somethin' more formal . . . Sage?"

"Oh cut that out Séamus! Nothing has changed. We're still friends and I'm still Dana. I'm Morrígan too, I guess, but still Dana. You'll still call me Dana or 'young one', okay?"

He laughs at me and hugs me goodbye.

"Aury, you ready to go home for a while?"

She zooms straight to my backpack and slides into her pocket. "I'm ready!" she squeaks.

I put my backpack on and hold my sketchbook out in front of me sketching the back porch and our Camelia bush in our back yard. Bébinn helps me sing and the drawing pops quicker than usual.

"I'll see you soon, Éire."

My heart aches as I close my eyes and I make the transition. Every time I pop into our yard like this I'm afraid to open my eyes, hoping against hope that neither of my parents are anywhere around.

Whew! I'm clear.

I round the front corner of the house and walk up the front steps and throw open the door. It feels like I've been gone forever!

"Mama! I'm home!" I yell. "Where are you?"

"We're in the Kitchen, D."

I put my backpack down at the bottom of the stairs and I see Aurelia slip out and zip upstairs to my room.

I jog back to the kitchen and throw my arms around my mama. "I missed you, Mom!" I say, squeezing her tight. "You too, Daddy!" I kiss him on the cheek.

"Dana? Is everything okay?" Daddy asks.

"Well yeah! What do you mean?"

Mama chimes in. "You're acting kind of funny." She stands back and looks at me, cocking her head to the side. She looks me up and down then, the question plastered on her face: "Is something different? You look . . . different."

"Uh . . . no? What would be different, Mama? I'm just in a good mood. I had a great weekend with my friends."

Not a lie. I smile at how great it feels to be able to tell the truth for once.

"Well that's good! I'm glad you had a good time!" Mama says looking at Daddy with a look that says: 'Wow, she's finally doing something normal and having fun instead of moping around the house!'

"So, did we get any mail on Saturday?" I ask.

"Yeah, but nothing from the College if that's what you're asking after," Dad says.

"Aww man! Wish something from them would hurry up and get here already!"

"Well Christmas is next week, I'm sure they'll get their acceptances out before then, so that new students can start at the beginning of the second semester."

"Ugh! Well, I wonder if that means I didn't get in? I mean, maybe I'm not getting an acceptance if I haven't gotten anything yet . . ." I put on my best down-in-the-dumps face.

"Now Dana. You're just going to have to be patient," Mama says.

"Yeah . . . I know." I pause for a moment in thought. "I think I'm going to paint for a while this afternoon guys."

I head for the stairs. "Love you!"

"We love you too, D," they say in unison.

Upstairs with Aurelia looking on, for the first time in weeks, I do just what I told my parents I was. I paint for no other reason than to create a painting. I don't bring anything to life, I don't go anywhere. I just watch the brush wash paint over the surface of the paper and it feels so good.

I check the mail Monday, Tuesday and Wednesday but nothing comes for me. Christmas is Thursday and I spend it with my Mom and Dad appreciating their company, knowing that soon I won't be able to see them just any old time I want to.

It's hard to keep my secrets from them during the Holiday week because I'm around them constantly. My excitement at everything ahead wells up and threatens to spew out at the most inopportune times.

When I open the main gifts my parents got for me, a fancy smart phone and a brand new laptop, I nearly tell them how hard it's going to be for me to find time to use them.

How am *I going to use these things?*

I'm so distracted by the logistics of using the gifts once I'm living in the Otherworld, that I forget to be as excited as I should be.

I'll have to pop back to the Human World once a week to connect to the internet so I can turn in school work. I guess I'll just call my parents then. From New York! That way if they want to video chat or something . . . I can do this! It will work and Bébinn can go with me! She can be my new friend from school. This is going to be amazing!

I snap back to the present just in time to see the disappointment on my Daddy's face.

I jump up and hug and kiss them both, just to see him smile. "Thank you so much! What a great Christmas this is! I love you!"

On Saturday I roll out of bed before I'm really even fully awake.

"Aury! Today is the day! I know it. My acceptance letter is coming *today*!"

I jump up and scurry around getting ready and run downstairs, leaving Aurelia surfing the internet - her morning routine.

In the kitchen Daddy is cooking.

"Ha! Giving Mama a break, huh?" I tease.

"Yeah, I thought I'd give it a shot anyway," he replies good-naturedly.

"Well when you're done . . . ahem . . . '*cooking*'," I wink at Mama who is sitting at the counter drinking her coffee, "Can you take me to the Post Office, please? I've got a good feeling about today. My acceptance is going to come today, I just know it!"

Daddy laughs at my joke. "Sure, honey. I'll take you as soon as we finish eating."

"Okay, Dad, thanks!"

We sit down and eat together and I have a great time joking and laughing with them. We're all in a great mood and I can tell they've noticed that I'm feeling good.

We finish up and Dad stands up. "Well, let's get going, D! I've got a good feeling about today too," he smiles at me and even the twinge of guilt I feel can't spoil my morning.

I kiss my mom on the cheek. "Can I do the dishes when we get back?"

"Go! I got 'em today," she says.

"Thanks, Mama," I call from the hall as I put on my coat and walk out the door with my dad. On the porch I notice a couple of crows pecking at the grass in the yard.

So weird that I know those are not just ordinary crows, but my Dad doesn't. It's like we're already living in two separate worlds. For now, I put all that aside in my head and concentrate on what's happening today, not where I'm going or why.

In the car he turns to me and looks me squarely in the face.

"Dana, I'm so glad to see you feeling so much better," and all my guilt washes away surprisingly.

If my dad likes to see me happy and what I'm doing makes me happy, truly happy, then why feel bad?

I smile from ear to ear. "Yes, I am feeling much better, Daddy. I don't feel so lost anymore."

Now that I'm found.

He pulls away from the curb and we ride to the Post Office in silence. Despite knowing that acceptance letters are definitely coming, the anticipation of *when* they're coming makes me feel genuinely nervous.

When we get there, I reach into the glove compartment to get the box key and jump out of the car.

"Be right back," I say flashing my daddy a big toothy grin.

I walk into the Post Office, straight to our box and when I get there, I put my hand on the door and visualize the letters inside, singing a song soft and low under my breath.

If they aren't going to show up on their own, I'll make them show up! I turn the key and close my eyes tight for a moment, then open them and peer inside. There's a decent sized pile of mail in the box and I pull it out. I'm so nervous I can't even go through it. I hurry back to the car with the mail.

Inside the car I thrust the pile at my dad.

"Daddy, I can't do it. You look. Please?"

He laughs at me and takes the pile of mail. He rifles through it and holds up two envelopes dropping the rest in his lap.

"Dana," he calls in a sing-song voice. "I've got two envelopes here from the College with your name on them! Shall I do it, or do you want to?"

"No, you do it, Dad. I can't. My stomach is in crazy knots." It's not a lie.

He rips into the envelopes one at a time, reading them quickly, a smile forming across his lips that grows bigger with each line he reads.

Suddenly my guilt is unbearable!

Oh my God, Dad . . . don't get that excited. I don't think I can keep lying if you get that *excited!*

"Well, honey . . ." he looks at me with his giant, guilt-inducing grin. "You did it! YOU GOT IN!" He ends the sentence in his roaring, excited, yelling voice.

I give him the best smile I can muster considering that inside I feel like a big fat liar and I hope I can play it off as nerves.

"And the best part is, it looks like you got a scholarship as well!" he exclaims. "I didn't even know you applied for one! And here I've been worrying all these weeks about how we were going to pay for this!

Let's get these home to show your Mom!"

He hands me the letters with the other mail and speeds off toward home obviously excited. Its impossible not to laugh at his enthusiasm.

When we get back to our house he grabs up the letters and takes my hand, dragging me into the house where I have to do my best acting job for my mom.

Oh man, I'll be glad when this is over with.

"Let's celebrate!" Mama squeals. She walks to the kitchen and we follow after her. She reaches into the refrigerator and pulls out a bottle of champagne. "I bought this for New Year's Eve, but what the hay, I say we open it right now!"

"Mama!" I laugh nervously. "It's like 11 o'clock in the morning!"

"So what?! It's not every day your daughter gets into college!"

I can't hold back the floodgate of emotions that pour over me and my mood falls, my face falls.

"Mama . . . I can't." I can't tear my eyes away from the bottle of champagne.

She looks from me to the bottle and quickly realizes

what's happened.

"Oh Dana! I'm so sorry," she stashes it back in the refrigerator as fast as she can. I smile weakly remembering the scenes of my darkest day for the first time in weeks.

"It's okay, Mama," but I am reduced to tears and she is left feeling guilty. She walks over to me slowly and wraps me in a bear hug, breaking down right along with me. Daddy just stands in the doorway looking at the two of us in bewilderment.

"Dana, this is supposed to be a happy day . . ." she whispers gently.

I sniffle and wipe at my eyes, straightening up. "I know."

Screw him! I'm not going to let that idiot ruin my day today!

"Really, I'm okay. Let's look at flights, okay?"

"Yeah," Daddy says, "Let's do that!" I can tell he's relieved to have something to do now. He makes me giggle.

We all peruse travel sites together comparing flights and times and I convince them to let me fly out on Tuesday, which isn't hard since that day has the best fares. They purchase my ticket, which I'll not be using, and I jump up excited again.

"Okay, gotta go pack! That's only three days away!"

I spend the next three days doing laundry, deciding what I should take and what I should leave, packing bags and unpacking them to rearrange things to get more in. I eat dinners and breakfasts with my parents, savoring every moment, and I lay in bed at night talking with Aurelia about all the things we're going to do. We dream together about living in the Otherworld full time.

Monday night I lay awake in bed long after Aurelia

has gone to sleep thinking of Bébinn and our friends in the Otherworld.

I can't wait to get back. I wish I could talk to Bébinn and tell her I'm coming back tomorrow.

I fall asleep thinking of my sister and all the adventures we'll have together. I wonder about our adventures as the Morrígan and Éire.

I'll bet we got in a lot of trouble together.

When my eyes open it's because my tiny faerie alarm clock is poking my cheek chiming: "Get up, get up, we're moving today!"

I lay there staring at the ceiling for a minute or two.

Today is going to be great, but difficult. Somehow I have to convince my parents that I get on a plane without actually getting on a plane.

I sit up feeling overwhelmed by my feelings. I'm headed for the unknown and it's exciting, but leaving my parents and the safety and comfort of our home is scary.

"Aury, I'll be back in just a little bit. Can I get you some fruit for breakfast today?"

"Mmm! Pineapple? Do we have any left? It was so good!"

"I'll check," I giggle.

I walk downstairs still in my pajamas and both my parents are in the kitchen preparing breakfast. There's pancakes, eggs, bacon, sausage, hash browns and fresh-squeezed orange juice.

"It smells delicious, you guys! I'm going to miss your cooking, Mama!" I say hugging her. She hugs me back really tight for a long time.

"Today's your big day," she says.

"Yep!"

"Excited?" Daddy asks.

"Yep!" I repeat laughing.

"We need to leave for the airport around 8:30," he reminds me. "You all set to go?"

"Yep, got my bags all packed."

"Okay, then. Let's eat," Mama chimes in. I get the feeling she doesn't want to talk about my impending departure.

We sit down and enjoy our last family meal together for the foreseeable future, our conversation light and happy. We do the dishes together immediately after and I root through the refrigerator looking for the pineapple I cut up a day or two ago. When I find it, I take a couple of pieces out of the container, pop one in my mouth, and take a couple back upstairs with me for Aurelia.

Pineapple is one of my favorite fruits too so we share the pieces when I make it back to my room. It's a quick snack, because I have to start taking my bags down to put in the car. I stand over them going through my mental checklist, taking a walk through various rooms of our house making sure I'm not leaving anything I'll need.

It's not like they can just mail me something I forgot.

I put my coat on, put my backpack on my back with Aurelia in her mesh pocket and lug my bags down to the front door where my dad takes over the job of packing the trunk.

I stand with him while he does it.

"Listen, Dad? I think it will be best if you guys just drop me off at check-in. There's no need to drag out our good-byes all morning long while I wait in line and check bags and everything. I'll handle all that on my own and that way you guys won't have to park."

"Are you sure, Dana?"

"Yeah, I think it might be easier on me actually if we

just say our good-byes at the curb, no lingering."

"Okay, if that's what you want, we can do it that way. It will probably be better for Mom that way too, actually."

"Thanks, Daddy," I smile, relieved. Now I don't have to worry about how the heck to go through the check-in line, but keep my bags with me.

Mama, emerges from our front door and walks up to stand right in front of me. She's teary-eyed. She puts a hand on each shoulder holding me out in front of her as if to take one last long look at me. She smiles, her red, watery eyes squinting and roaming over my face and my hair.

"Wow, this is cool, Dana. Where'd you get it?" she asks.

Oh no . . .

She reaches to pick up the key before I can stop her and as her fingers close around its shaft, it sparks and she jerks her hand back. The sparks and discomfort seem to serve as a distraction so she doesn't notice that the key actually flies out of her hand as well.

"Ouch!" she says shaking her hand. "It shocked me!"

"Oh," I laugh nervously, tucking the key back into my shirt where it usually stays, "I just found it at an antique store and I liked it so I put it on a necklace cord, Mama."

Must have fallen out of my shirt when I bent over to pick up bags. That was a close one.

"We need to get going, ladies," Daddy says.

Mama hugs me again and we duck into the car. I carry my backpack on my lap with Aurelia's mesh pocket facing me.

The ride to the airport seems like the longest car ride of my life. The music on the radio drifts into and out of my thoughts, but I don't hear most of it. My mind is already in the Otherworld.

After what seems like days, Dad takes the exit and starts to get in the drop-off lane and Mama gives him a confused look.

"Dana thought it would be better to just drop her off at the curb at check-in. You know? Not prolong the good-byes?"

"No," she says matter-of-factly. "It's bad enough we're not taking her to New York. I am going as far as I can with her in the airport."

Well, that's that.

Her tone of voice tells me that it would be futile to argue. My mother has a mind like a steel trap. Once it's locked down on some idea, it's nearly impossible to pry it open.

Now what? Go through ticketing, get on the plane and once I'm in New York pop to the Otherworld? I can't take Aurelia through security . . .

Dad knows it's pointless too. He steers the car to the lane for the airport parking garage. We park and silently haul my bags from the trunk to check-in. My nerves are getting the best of me and Mama is just being stubborn. Poor Daddy is caught in the middle.

The check-in line is long and excruciating. Waiting with my parents while I continue in this great, big lie is much more than I was prepared for today. I thought the active lying part would come to an end when I got out of our car.

We get through it finally, I check my bags, keep my backpack, and we head for security. When I spot the restrooms I make a quick break away.

"Hey guys, I need to make a stop in the little girls'

room quick before I go through security, ok?"

They smile and nod and I disappear through the door.

Inside I find a stall so I can whisper to Aurelia who's still in her tiny pocket.

"Aury!" I hiss. "I can't take you through security. What should we do?"

"I can just go ahead and pop over to the Otherworld to wait for you there. I'll go straight to Séamus's house, that way you don't have to worry about hiding me."

"Okay, I think that's a good idea."

She flies close to my face and gives me one of her amazing faerie hugs and kisses my cheek.

Works every time.

It calms my frazzled nerves right away.

"Have a safe trip and keep your eyes peeled!" She chirps, and a second later she's gone.

Never seen her do that before, pretty neat!

I give myself a few minutes in the bathroom so it appears that I had a legitimate reason to go in and then emerge feeling relieved.

Mama and Daddy are waiting for me with smiles on their faces. Mama's smile continues to look strange like a pair of comedy and tragedy theater masks oddly melded into one, looking like a sad, happy smile.

"Well this is where we part," I say trying to sound as upbeat as I can even though I am a little sad as well.

We hug, and she kisses my cheek then launches into the last absurd conversation we'll have for a while. I happily indulge her crazy questions one last time as she quizzes me about what I brought, if I have everything I'll need. She tells me to be careful in New York, to be sure I lock my door, and to call frequently.

"How about we talk on Sundays, Mom? Let's settle on

that ahead of time, okay?"

She smiles brightly at me in confirmation, and I can see the mixed emotions in her eyes.

"Dana, I just want you to know that I'm proud of you. I will miss you desperately, but I know this is what you need to do," she hugs me like she thinks if she holds me there longer, I might change my mind and stay with her. For a moment I almost think I might.

"I love you, Mama," I cast my eyes downward, ashamed that she's proud of me while I'm lying through my teeth, but not so ashamed that I can stay. I'm hurtling ever forward these days, toward a destiny I never asked for, but the path feels right, and the momentum is set on auto-pilot with no off switch.

I break free and step sideways to stand in front of my daddy. I look at him standing there, smiling broadly, and my resolve falters again. If anyone or anything could flip the off switch, it would be my daddy. I can see that he is trying bravely to hide tears welling up in his eyes, so I quickly hug him, whispering in his ear:

"I'll always be my daddy's girl. Love you, Dad."

"I love you too, D," his emotions show on his face and it clearly makes him uncomfortable. "You'd better hurry up, that security line looks like a doozy."

I step back and take a quick last look at them both, waving silently.

I hope I see you again.

Turning away from them, I heave a great sigh and walk toward the security line with a heavy heart. Even though I know I'm walking this new path straight into what will only be the greatest adventure of my life, it's hard not to feel the pangs of guilt and sadness that come from leaving home for the first time.

I push those feelings to the back of my mind, though, because I've never traveled alone before and there's a lot to think about. I realize I have to concentrate on the task at hand.

The long line of people standing impatiently, taking off shoes and coats, stuffing their things into plastic bins shuffling along on conveyor belts, pulling electronics out of their bags, chatting amongst themselves, moves slower than slow. It *creeps* along and I would just slip out, go into a restroom stall, and draw Séamus's house, but checking my bags committed me to this flight! Besides that, my parents stand just outside of the barricade watching me, smiling and waving every time I glance their way. There's no way I can go anywhere but through.

It's finally my turn at the conveyor belt. I take care of my belongings and look up at the metal detector as I go through it. No alarm sounds, but a voice comes to me through the din of the activity of the area.

When I look at the security guard who spoke, my heart stops.

The Templar from the Metropolitan, the same man from my dream, and the streets of Fourknocks, stands directly in front of me in full security guard uniform.

"Come with me," he says, but I just stare at him wide-eyed, in disbelief. "Ma'am?" he says a bit louder. "I said you need to come with me." His gold, stamped ring glares at me like an evil eye and his voice is grating and stern.

I'm panicking trying to think of a way out of this.

If I put up a fight, my parents will be alerted that something is wrong and then the game is up, it'll all be over. If I don't, what's going to happen to me?

I have no choice but to go. I give a quick, last wave to

my parents, plaster on the absolute best fake smile I can muster, and grab my stuff as it comes through the x-ray machine. With my backpack in hand, I follow the Templar through security. We go through a door and he reaches for my upper arm, holding it in a vice grip, and there it is again. The feeling that I've met him before. It's deep down in my consciousness somewhere, in a place I can barely access.

He takes me down a side hallway away from the safety of the hustle and bustle of the public crowd, into the danger of seclusion.

He is silent as we go. After a few minutes of traveling down dim hallways he leads me through a door into the bright light of day out onto the tarmac.

"Where are you taking me?!" I yell loudly trying to get someone's attention, but the noise of the planes is too loud and the people working are too spread out, no one hears.

"You have a date with the Pope." he says calmly, but doesn't look at me.

"The Pope? Why are you taking me to see the Pope?"

He is silent, obviously ignoring my question.

I realize nothing I say will entice this stoic figure to tell me what's going on, but my heart is beating wildly and my breath is ragged like I've run five miles. He is guiding me toward a plane on the tarmac away from everything else. I frantically search for someone to call out to; someone to catch my eye that I can convince to help me, but there's no one else around. The plane is a small jet out on its own.

What the hell am I going to do?

Just when I think all hope is lost, he loosens his grip on my arm when the door of the plane sticks briefly and I seize the opportunity. I bolt, running as fast as my little legs can carry me, but we're not in a city full of people this time. There's nothing in his way and he catches me quickly. I feel a deafening blow on the back of my head, my knees buckle, and blackness creeps in on all sides of my vision like curtains until the windows of my eyes are covered.

When I wake, I'm disoriented.

Where am I?

I put my hand to the back of my head where I feel a knot throbbing like it's got a small hammer behind it, threatening to break through at any moment. The ache has spread to encompass my whole head, making it hard to put together complete thoughts. There's dried blood caked in my hair.

I squint my eyes and look around me. There are seats lining walls with small, funny windows and a large man sitting in one of the seats across from me.

A plane?

Realization dawns . . .

The Templar, the plane, going to see the Pope . . . going to see the Pope?

The question still resounds in my aching skull.

Oh Aury, I'm glad you didn't stay with me.

My head hurts too badly to try to think of what I'm going to do to get out of this mess. I close my eyes and sleep overtakes me once again.

CHAPTER TEN

Audience with the Pope

I'm in my Otherworld meadow, head still pounding, but I can at least think clearly. Bébinn is standing with me.

"Éire, you've got to find me. I've been kidnapped by the Templar. He told me that he's taking me to Rome to see the Pope, but I don't know why. Please, Sister, you've got to get to me. I don't think I'll be able to get away without help."

"Morrígan, I'll be there. I won't let you be taken from me again."

She wraps her arms around me and kisses me on the forehead and the warmth from her lips finds its way around my head, the pain at the base of my skull subsiding immediately.

When I wake from this dream, my head is clear and the pain is actually gone. I'm ready to face my newest problem head on, but for now, since I'm trapped in this flying prison, the only thing I can do is observe my captor.

I feel the Flower of Awareness open once again and the part of me that is the Morrígan knows I need to look him over and take in every detail. The only way to defeat this man is to know him. Morrígan knows I need to note his strengths and his weaknesses; try to use them to build a picture of his character and his life. Maybe something in that picture will be able to help me plan a way out of this.

My eyes rove over him, hungry to see everything there is to see, noting that he is quiet and seemingly contemplative, staring out a window of the plane.

He's a thinker?

This thinker has broad shoulders and big hands and feet. His marred face is sectioned by deep, slashing scars, and framed by a large, square jaw. His small eyes and beakish nose, a roman nose, make him appear bird-like, but not unattractive.

This man is dangerous - the flower tells me - he has seen many battles and won many. He is tough, able to survive things most are not.

His taste in clothing tells me that he is wealthy; the Vatican must pay him handsomely. He has changed out of his security guard uniform into a pair of dark brown, flat-front trousers, a cream, collared shirt, and a sleek, black, leather jacket. His square-toed leather shoes are stamped with intricate designs. They look expensive.

Of course, Italian leather. Not that it's relevant. My mind is wandering.

He stands without looking in my direction allowing me to continue my study undetected as he walks out of the cabin of the plane we are in.

As he does I notice something I haven't noticed before: he walks with a slight limp. I'm positive he didn't have it earlier.

Maybe running to catch me affected him somehow? An injury

that is aggravated by running? A bad knee, perhaps?

I make a mental note to observe that more closely while I look around my environment again, determined to see something I missed before that might help me, but I am quickly disappointed. My backpack is across the room, and I am handcuffed to the bench seat I'm lying on.

If only I could get to it. I could draw myself right out of this situation. But I guess this guy is not necessarily big and dumb. He's seen what I can do with my sketchbook. Don't suppose he'll make the mistake of letting me keep my stuff so I can do it again.

When I'm sure there's nothing I can do to help myself in my current predicament, I decide that a long trip to Europe on a plane with nothing to do except worry is best spent sleeping. My stressed-out body could use the rest to prepare for whatever it is I'll face in Rome.

I close my eyes again, but this time my sleep is dreamless and heavy. I am mentally and physically exhausted and sleep comes like a welcome vacation.

What seems like moments later though, I am jolted awake by the jerk of the plane touching down and the lack of transition out of sleep leaves my stomach churning and my heart racing once again. My captor is in his seat again, buckled in, and watching me. His gaze is focused on some part of my body, which frays my nerves even further. Being completely vulnerable in the presence of a large, powerful man is not something I ever wanted to feel again.

His eyes meet mine and his cheeks color slightly. He sets his face back to the rigid stone mask that belies no emotion and turns away quickly.

A weakness for women - the Flower of Understanding speaks in my head in my own voice, but the thoughts clearly come from Morrígan. I feel her wisdom rise up in me more and more frequently. Her spirit is always close to the surface of mine now.

Bet the Church would love to know about that.

The plane comes to a stop and the Templar stands and walks toward me. He reaches into his pocket and takes out a tiny key to unlock my handcuffs. He removes them from around the plane bench and cuffs one on his wrist, leaving the other on mine.

His presence so close to me makes the hair on the back of my neck stand up. He's like a wall that threatens to hem me in.

We exit the plane swiftly and he drags me along the tarmac of a new airport. It's small and there are no large, commercial jets anywhere around; not many people, either. I have to assume we are in Italy now.

Pretty crazy in this day and age that someone could travel to another country without once showing a passport. Wonder if this is a private airport?

The Pope's private plane and his private airport - the Morrígan tells me.

I notice that the Templar is still slightly limping, although not as much as he was earlier. He takes me directly to a limousine and hauls me into the back seat with him. The start of a plan forms in the back of my mind.

When he glances my way after we are inside the car I smile at him meekly and he looks confused. He dismissively turns away and spends the brief car ride looking out the window. I do the same.

I watch the streets of Rome fly by losing myself in the scenery. There are gorgeous buildings of every color lining bumpy, cobblestone streets. We pass the

Colosseum and a strange area of ruins in a grassy field where there are columns laying down and some standing up. It all looks like a big, jumbled mess. We pass beautiful fountains containing huge, masterful sculptures.

I watch the people walking on the sidewalks and in the streets and I wonder about their lives and their stories; about their histories and ancestry.

Where are they going? Where did they come from? How many are tourists and how many are Romans?

So much of the world was influenced thousands of years ago by the government that originated in this city. This fact exponentially multiplies the amazement I feel being here.

The limo stops and I snap back to my reality when the Templar tugs at my wrist with the handcuffs. I hurry and scramble out of the car door to avoid being dragged out and falling down. Despite being annoyed at the rough treatment I try to put on a brave face and smile at him again.

If he likes women so much, I'll make him like me. Maybe I'll be able to use that . . .

"What's your name?" I ask him, but he doesn't reply.

I just shrug and continue on. "Well, whatever. My name is Dana." I walk faster to keep up with him and move closer to his side so that the chain on the handcuffs has a little slack and my hand and arm brushes his.

He looks down at me with something like curiosity in his eyes, but only briefly. He quickly regains his wits and puts the stony face back into place once again.

"Look," I say to him peering up into his giant face, "We can do this the hard way, or we can be civil and try to get along."

He keeps his eyes fixed forward while we shuffle on

and doesn't speak to me or look at me.

In frustration, which I try my hardest to keep hidden, I turn my attention back to the direction we're walking and continue on in silence. Just ahead there's a large, yellow building with a big, wooden door, and I note how remarkably like the door at Bébinn's house it is.

He walks me up to the door and knocks loudly.

"Lorenzo," he says without looking in my direction.

His voice startles me, but I regain my composure and slowly turn to face him, smiling.

There now, we've made friends. I stifle a shudder.

The door opens and a man in a black beret and an eye-catching, brightly colored uniform greets Lorenzo. I'm distracted briefly by what he is wearing. Both the pants and top seem to be made up of strips of cloth in royal purple and gold with another layer in red fabric underneath. The strips run vertically and form a poof just below the knees and elbows. He wears long socks in the same vertical stripe pattern in the same colors.

How bizarre. What is *this guy?*

He ushers us into the building and leads us through a couple of grand, ornately decorated rooms. He stops in one of the larger ones and gestures to a small antique sofa. It is trimmed in woodwork that has been gilded, and the thought occurs to me that this whole place looks like it was built for a king. The walls are lined with enormous paintings in thick frames and intricate tapestries depicting hunting scenes and farmers in fields harvesting crops. The furniture all looks like something from a history book trimmed with beautifully carved details and oversized rugs line the marble floors.

Lorenzo sits on the small couch and I quickly sit next to him. I am trying to be as cooperative as I can, or at least give the impression that I am - hoping to build some level of rapport with him, so I'm careful to be sure he isn't having to drag me around.

The oddly-dressed man in the black beret says a few words to my captor in Italian and exits the room swiftly in a flurry of pattern and color.

Once again I'm left alone with this giant of a man. He's sitting too close to me and I hate the way it feels, but I know I have to move past that. If I am going to get him to trust me enough to let me have a bit of freedom, I need to lay it on thick, and being afraid of him isn't going to allow me to do that.

After a few more minutes of awkward silence, a man dressed in a crisp suit strolls into the room. We stand up.

"Lorenzo!" he bellows walking straight to the giant Templar, taking him by the shoulders, kissing him on both cheeks. "Welcome back to Roma!"

The man speaks English.

He must be doing that for my benefit. My bitterness at being held captive resurfaces despite my best efforts to keep it at bay. *How polite of him.*

"Miss Walker." He looks me over from head to toe, eyes widening when he spots the handcuffs.

His face screws up into a look of distaste. "Lorenzo! Was this really necessary?" he asks as he hooks a finger under the chain of the handcuffs, lifting them up, in turn lifting our hands with them.

"She tried to run, Sir," he replies.

The man turns back to me with a genteel smile. "That's not going to be a problem here, is it Miss Walker? We can take these off, can't we?"

I blink up at him, shocked by his willingness to let me out of the handcuffs, but more importantly by the fact that he knows my name.

He looks back at Lorenzo and nods his head in the direction of the handcuffs without a sound. The Templar immediately releases me and I breathe a sigh of relief, rubbing my wrist.

"Miss Walker, welcome to the Papal Apartments. Our newest Pope prefers the modesty of the Vatican Guest House, so you'll be staying here. My name is Patrizio Borghi and I'll be your host while you stay with us here. Let's show you to your room and get you settled in, shall we? I hope you'll be pleased with the accommodations."

He takes a few steps and I am just starting to follow when another man wearing the colorful uniform pops into the room holding my backpack.

Patrizio motions for us to wait where we are and goes to the doorway to talk to the uniformed man.

I didn't even realize I didn't have it!

My host comes back to where he left us, extends the backpack toward me and my heart skips a beat in anticipation.

My way out!

"Here's your bag," he says smoothly, "But your sketchbooks and pencils have been removed, my dear. I'm sure you understand."

I nod again, visibly disappointed and completely devastated.

"Follow me," he says.

I glance at Lorenzo, sure that this will be the last time I see him for a while, but when we start walking he follows!

Great, he really is going to be my 'friend' here. I'm unable to suppress the eye roll that forces its way out.

I really must *stop doing that!*

Patrizio takes us on a winding tour of the gorgeous apartments. The multitude of turns down new hallways and into big rooms and small rooms squashes any idea I have of escaping . . . from this building at least. It's so large and maze-like, I'm fairly sure I wouldn't be able to find my way back out.

I'll have to figure out a way to get Lorenzo to take me outside.

We finally turn down a long hallway, the longest on the tour, and stop outside of one of its large doors. There's a lovely Queen Anne chair positioned to the left of the door.

My host produces a skeleton key from his pocket, unlocks the door, and swings it open, stepping back to allow me to see inside. I stand rooted in the doorway unable to move.

The view is breathtaking. The room is so beautiful that for a moment I forget I'm a prisoner here. I feel more like a princess.

"Well, Miss Walker? How do you like it?"

"It's magnificent," I say, feeling like a sell-out, but the little girl in me that played dress up and imagined growing up and living in a castle spoke before I could stop her.

You can't like this! It's all a part of some crazy master plan. Get a grip, Dana. Don't allow yourself to be sucked in.

"Please," Patrizio gestures into the room, urging me forward. "Go in, make yourself at home, and get comfortable. I think you'll find it quite cozy.

Lorenzo will be right outside if you need anything and he will escort you to the evening meal. Tomorrow you will meet with the Pope."

He turns to Lorenzo. "Miss Walker is our guest, Lorenzo. Please make her comfortable and treat her appropriately. No more handcuffs."

"As you wish, Sir."

I walk forward into the room I'm to stay in for the duration of my imprisonment, and Patrizio closes the door behind me.

"Ciao, Miss Walker."

I hear the key rattle in the door and a distinct click as he locks me inside. I stand where I stopped and sigh heavily. I swallow and the feeling of being all alone makes its way down my throat into my empty belly like a bitter medicine, settling in and making me feel queasy.

I miss Aurelia, but I'm so glad she isn't here to go through all of this. I long for my parents' protection and lament my lies. They have no idea where I am or that I'm in danger.

I really hope Bébinn gets here soon.

Morrígan interjects and makes herself known.

It will do us no good to wallow in the negative aspects of the situation, you'll only get bogged down in the mire and miss important observations because you're distracted.

I know she's right, so I stash away my fear like dirt swept under the rug, and I turn my attention to the room.

The first thing that catches my eye is a wall of books, and upon inspecting it a little closer, I am pleasantly surprised to see that they've stocked it with books in English! All my favorites are here as well as several that I have always wanted to read, but haven't gotten around to. One whole shelf is lined with the classics, several that I've read, but many, many that I haven't.

There's a couch and a chaise lounge and a couple other small chairs situated into a sitting area fit for conversation.

There's a window in this room and I push aside the floor to ceiling, heavy curtains and watch the people in the street below. It looks like there's some kind of market just a street over. I can see into part of it.

On the left-hand wall is a doorway.

Wonder what's in there?

I walk to it and can see that there is a small walk way that opens up into a beautiful bedroom with a door just inside, also to the left, that leads into a powder room.

I smile at how easy it is to get lost in the finery of this place and forget that my life is turned upside down right now.

Ambling through the tiny walkway into the powder room, I trail my hand along the wall and across the cold, marble counter top in front of a mirror that extends all the way to the ceiling. There's yet another door inside this room, leading to the biggest bathroom I've ever seen. Opposite the door is an antique bathtub encased in paneled mahogany. The same large, trimmed panels line the lower half of the walls and appear to flow off the wall and around the tub. The large rounded lip of the bathtub extends over the edges of the wood panel encasement.

There is an old fashioned water closet toilet in a small room in this main room of the bathroom also.

This place looks like time has failed to march on.

It has been modernized in some ways, like indoor plumbing and electricity, but in other ways, it's like time has been standing still for the last hundred years.

On to the bedroom.

Against the far wall is a giant, four-post bed clothed in luxurious linens. The duvet is made of damask with scenes woven into it similar to the tapestries I saw when I first arrived. The posts of the bed are the size of logs, carved with a twist along their entire length. A heavy canopy of similar fabric adorns the bed, and the large, floor to ceiling windows on either side have curtains and valences made of the same fabric the duvet is made of.

The walls of the room are painted a deep, rich, brick red color and the glossy lacquered floor of this room is scattered with large, red rugs. The room has an antique secretary and I open all the drawers, hoping I might get lucky and find a writing utensil inside, but the drawers are completely empty.

They're no dummies.

My mind wanders back to the books on the shelf and I walk back to the sitting room to peruse them a little more thoroughly. It isn't long before I spot a copy of Lewis Carrol's Alice in Wonderland and think to myself how much I feel like Alice right about now. So I pull it off the shelf and wander around the couch and sit down on the chaise lounge.

I wonder who has sat on this before me . . .

I make myself comfortable, open the book, and start to read, but soon my mind is wandering, thinking about the Otherworld and Séamus, my sister, my faerie. Before long I am opening my sleepy eyes to the *lovely* face of Lorenzo, his low, gruff voice jerking me out of sleep once again.

"Wake up. Time for the evening meal."

Suppose I'd better get used to that for the time being.

A flash of the dream I had weeks ago of dying in a church, comes back to me. The face that was crying . . . was his! He was looking down at me in almost the exact same way he is now. Somehow I had forgotten that detail in the confusion of things.

Strange . . .

"Okay," I say feeling completely baffled by the realization. I sit up and stretch, trying to shake the oddity of the connection between my dream and this moment.

"Can you excuse me please? I need to freshen up," . . . *and be alone with my thoughts for a minute.*

He stands up straight and turns, stalking out of the room with a huff.

Doesn't like me asking him to leave my room. Noted - weird, but noted.

I walk to the powder room and splash cold water on my face to try to help wake up fully and hopefully relieve any puffiness from the trip and my nap.

What can that mean? Lorenzo was crying in my dream . . . I must be wrong. Rude, grumpy, stalker, creeper Lorenzo?

I search the drawers under the counter and find a new toothbrush and toothpaste and give my teeth a quick once over.

When I'm satisfied that I'm not smelly, I knock on the door to my room.

"Lorenzo, I'm ready."

The key clicks in the lock and the door opens to allow me to go through.

"You'll be wise not to try anything tricky," he says with a thick accent. "Don't force my hand within these walls."

I look at him with a new curiosity. *Why was he crying? It just doesn't make sense!* "I promise, I will behave perfectly." I say seriously, blinking up at him, and when our eyes meet he holds my gaze.

His eyes look hungry. I've seen that look before on the plane when he didn't know I was looking, but when he caught my eye then, he quickly looked away. This time he doesn't. The longing is blatant, but there seems to be something more in it than I thought.

You know him. . . - chimes the Morrígan in my head.

I'm the one that breaks the connection finally when I start to feel a small charge from the prolonged interaction.

What was that? My stomach turns at the thought of my body's natural reaction to his obvious attraction.

Lorenzo turns away from me and starts walking down the long hallway. He clears his throat.

"Let's get going." The edge in his voice is gone. He's less gruff and sounds almost kind.

What did he see in my *eyes, I wonder?*

I follow him and we make our way through the maze, again turning so many times I can't count and can't even begin to form a mental map of the place. We finally arrive at a large dining room, housing a table that must be at least twenty feet long. Several people are already seated at the table, including Patrizio, but they rise from their chairs as I enter the room. I hover in the entrance unsure what to do.

Lorenzo gently places his hand at the small of my back as if to steady me, and the pressure of it resting there spurs me into action, but not before I take note of the tingle it sends through me. However mildly distracting it is, I force my mind to stay in the moment, consciously shifting my focus to what I'm doing here.

Every eye in the room is trained on me and I feel self conscious and young, underdressed, and slightly unworthy to be here. I nod to the other diners and they smile and nod back to me.

"May I introduce to you, Miss Dana Walker. She is a guest of the Pope and we're hoping she will enjoy her extended stay with us." Patrizio casts his eyes around the room.

I nod to several of them and they nod to me again, smiling, wearing looks of curiosity.

Just remember your Southern manners, Dana, and you'll be fine.

"Thank you. It's a pleasure to make your acquaintances." I add.

Lorenzo guides me to a chair next to Patrizio, pulls it out and gestures to the seat, indicating for me to sit down. I sit and he pushes it up to the table for me.

"Much better, Lorenzo," Patrizio winks in his direction.

My captor, guard, guide . . . *whatever he is* . . . walks around the table and sits in an empty chair directly across from mine. He catches my eye momentarily and for the first time since I've been here, shoots me a half smile as if to say 'Good job', which despite my best efforts, elicits a beaming grin from me. In spite of the scars that traverse his face, I am surprised to notice that Lorenzo is quite handsome when he smiles.

My inner voice of reason screeches.

Dana! What the hell are you doing? This man kidnapped you, hit you on the back of the head, and then looked at you like a pound of bacon he might gobble up when he thought you wouldn't see!

I close my eyes for a moment, trying to blink away those images and stay rooted in this room. Something is different. Maybe we've reached an understanding. Maybe I'm feeling less like a prisoner and more like a guest. Maybe it's a grand scheme to weaken my defenses, who knows?

All I know is that for the second time in five minutes he has made me feel like we're the only two people in the room.

Not good . . . but I like it.

An elegantly dressed, older lady addresses me. "Miss Walker, Patrizio tells us you're from America." It isn't a question, but I can tell I'm expected to treat it like one.

"Yes, that's correct," I reply.

"He also tells us you've been invited for a personal audience with the Pope. What an honor!"

"Yes ma'am, thank you. I do feel honored," I lie.

As honored as a prisoner forced to be here could feel . . . Bitterness seeps into my mood, but I press it back into the hole I buried it in earlier today.

Others around the table ask questions throughout the meal using polite terms and tones of voice, but it's obvious that their questions are designed to glean information without coming across as nosey.

I focus all my energy on listening intently to their questions and answer them to the best of my ability, at the same time enjoying the meal. The food is absolutely delicious, but I'm not surprised. I've always heard that eating authentic Italian food is an experience rather than just the menial task of eating.

Lorenzo doesn't talk at all during the dinner, and mostly only looks at his food. I see him push it around his plate like he either doesn't like it or is lost in thought. A couple of times I catch him stealing glances at me though. Each time his half smile makes him look sheepish.

When the final course is over, the other diners bid me and each other a good night and Patrizio instructs Lorenzo to see that I make it back to my room.

"Good night, Miss Walker," he says smiling, bowing slightly.

"Good night," I return.

Lorenzo and I make the walk back to my room in

silence, but about half way there curiosity gets the best of me and I allow my hand to brush his as we walk side by side. He stops and turns to face me with a look of consternation.

"Miss Walker . . . " his voice is low and pleading, but not unkind.

"I . . . I'm sorry," I say, and I am. I've obviously crossed some boundary and I'm as confused by the feelings I'm finding myself having in his presence as he is.

He turns away and I take that as my cue to leave him alone. I force myself to think of other things and put one foot in front of the other.

I'm a misguided idiot.

When we make it back to my door, he opens it up for me and I pass through it without looking at him again.

"Good night," I say into my empty rooms.

I hear a muffled "Good night" on the other side of the door as it closes and I decide the best thing for me will be sleep. For a split second I feel relief, but then remember that my bags have been lost. They're probably somewhere in New York and all my favorite clothes are inside them. I have no pajamas to wear to bed and no clean clothes to put on tomorrow.

I pad to the door as quietly as I can.

"Lorenzo?"

The lock clicks in the door and it opens once again and he stands in the doorway smiling at me with a big, dumb grin.

"How can I help you, Miss Walker?"

"Well . . . I don't have anything to wear to bed and it would be so nice to have my clothes laundered."

He walks through the doorway into the bedroom area. Curious, I follow him as he makes his way to a very large, ornate armoire and opens its doors. He smiles and takes my hand pulling me to stand in front of it and watches as my eyes widen in surprise.

The armoire has been filled with clothes for me. There are pajamas, jeans, t-shirts, hoodies and tennis shoes. There are also what one might describe as business attire, or dress-casual clothes: slacks, blazers, blouses. Some silky fabric in muted colors catches my eye and I touch it, pulling it out a little so I can see what it is.

Ball gowns? How long are they really planning to keep me here?

Lorenzo interrupts my thoughts. "Is there anything else you'll be needing tonight, Miss Walker?"

"I don't think so," I smile at him.

"Alright then," he hesitates, opens his mouth like he's going to say something, then shuts it again. "Good night."

He turns on his heel and exits the room quickly.

I smile inwardly. *What was that all about?*

As quickly as the thought comes, it goes and I am again entranced by my armoire full of new clothes. I reach for a pair of pajamas and pull a silky pair off its hanger. I can't wait to get a shower and put them on.

Hmm. What about undies?

I look for a drawer in the armoire and find some behind a door on the lower half, pull out the drawers and there's one full of conservative undies and another full of socks. I giggle a little.

Evidently the Pope doesn't approve of thong underwear. Go figure.

I gather up my new night clothes and take them into the bathroom where I pile them up on an upholstered bench sitting near the luxurious tub. I turn on the water, set it to a setting as hot as I can stand it, and search around for towels.

When that last detail is handled, I hang the towel on a hook on the wall behind the tub, strip down, and step in, enjoying the relaxing, hot water and the steam rising up to open the pores of the skin on my face.

The bath is so relaxing, in fact, that sleep threatens to close my eyelids fairly quickly.

I don't normally sleep so much, guess this has just been an exhausting day.

It seems crazy that I just waved good-bye to my parents this morning.

Not wanting to sleep in the bathtub I wash up and get out, slip into my silky, new PJs, brush my teeth and walk to my bed, but I stop before turning the covers back. Lorenzo creeps into my thoughts again, and the screeching voice of reason rears her ugly head again as well.

Dana, just get into bed and go to sleep. Don't go there. So I shake off the creeping Lorenzo, crawl under the covers, think to myself how marvelously soft the bed is, and fall asleep before that thought is even really finished.

The next morning I wake up gently, feeling invigorated and refreshed. I open my eyes to wonderful sunlight filling the room. Someone has pulled back the curtains?

I look around and Lorenzo is sitting on the bench at the foot of the bed watching me. It doesn't shock me that he's there. I almost expected it this morning. I lay there for a moment looking at him looking at me and wonder what he's thinking.

"Good morning," he finally says, softly, gently, wearing the signature half smile on his devilishly handsome face. It's such a contrast to his wake up call for dinner the night before, I'm stymied.

"Good morning," I say smiling back at him.

"It's time to go down to the dining room for breakfast."

"Do I have time to freshen up?"

"Yes, if you do it quickly. I didn't want to wake you this morning. You were sleeping more peacefully than I've seen you sleep for months." His face instantly takes on a look of alarm. He realizes his blunder.

". . . than you've seen me sleep for months . . .? What do you mean? You've been watching me sleep!" My voice rises in pitch as it tends to do when I am angry and he raises his hands, palms toward me, fingers spread in protest.

"Miss Walker, all will be clear today when you meet with the Pope. I promise, it's not what you think. At least it wasn't to begin with . . ."

I feel my face contort in anger, mixed with confusion, mixed with curiosity, mixed with pleasure all at the same time, which just makes for one big emotional mess in my head!

Anger seems to be the ruling emotion.

"Lorenzo, GET OUT! Please don't come in my room again uninvited! You can wake me up by knocking!"

"I'm sorry. It won't happen again." He again puts his hands up, but this time the gesture is sarcastic as if to say: "Fine! Have it your way!" He stands and backs away, then turns and stalks angrily out of the room again.

As soon as the door closes behind him, regret replaces my anger.

That *was a step backward in our friendship. What did he mean, 'at least not to begin with' . . .? What is all this? Who can I trust? Why am I upset that I was so harsh with him?* Why *do I* feel *like this? Why do I even care?*

I get up, get dressed and, brush my teeth and hair feeling grumpy and not in the mood to have to deal with something like seeing the Pope today.

Don't really have a choice, now do I?

With heavy heart and a lot of confusion I walk to the door and knock lightly.

"Lorenzo?"

The lock clicks and the door opens, but he stands to the side of the door not looking at me.

Who can blame him? I just bit his head off!

I step out, but as he reaches for the door I reach for his hand and touch it softly. He freezes where he stands.

I step in close to him, my hand still touching his, our faces inches from each other. Our eyes catch and hold.

"Lorenzo, I'm sorry. I can feel there's a lot happening here that I don't understand. I feel out of control and it upsets me. It's hard for me to be in this situation because of things that have happened before . . . "

But I don't get to finish my sentence because he silences my mouth with his. My eyes close and I breathe him in, the flower of understanding opening once again to tell me that this man is not what I've thought him to be. He is dangerous, yes, but not to me. And I *know* him. The Morrígan knows his touch, his breath. The two me's dwelling in my consciousness are both surprised.

The kiss goes on, my body electrifies, and my knees feel weak. My head begins to swim, knees start to buckle, but he wraps his arms around me and swoops me up, holding me to him, pressing the entire length of our bodies together.

My hands wind around his neck, finding his hair, I tangle my fingers in it pulling myself even closer. And then the screech starts in . . .

Dana! Stop! What are you doing?! You can't do this! You don't really *know who he is, he's just a man like all the rest, only wants one thing! He doesn't deserve it. He doesn't deserve you . . . like this!*

It gets to me and I tear away from him, breathless and panting, trying to catch my breath. I swipe at my lips with my sleeve, staring at him in wide-eyed indignation.

I don't know what to think or how to feel. He looks at me obviously hurt and confused and it breaks my heart and melts the ice that my screeching voice of reason builds up inside me at every opportunity.

I am so screwed up!

"Lorenzo," I plead. "I don't know what's happening. I don't know what I'm doing, what *we're* doing! Please explain what's going on. I'm so . . . confused." And with that my mixed emotions swell up and boil over and tears spill over with them, but I blubber on. "Yesterday you were . . . my enemy . . . someone I felt the need to escape from," my speech is punctuated with sobs, "But today . . . escape is the . . . last thing . . . I want . . . to do!"

He laughs quietly. "Women," he says shaking his head. He grabs me up again, tucks my head under his chin, and cradles me in big strong arms, one hand on the back of my head, the other on my back. I feel safer than I've ever felt in my life and I will my voice of reason to go jump in a lake. I shut it out, at least in terms of what's happening here with him, for good. I vow to let the Morrígan be my guiding voice from now on and she isn't putting up a fight about Lorenzo at all.

I raise my head and look up into his face. My entire body is on fire.

"What's happening, Lorenzo? Do you promise to

explain some of this to me tonight?"

"Yes," he says and kisses me lightly again, "I promise, but right now we have to get you to the dining room before they come looking for us.

"Okay, you're right." I take a deep breath, test my jelly legs, and pull myself together.

I'm doing a lot of this lately, pulling it together.

"Before you lock that," I say as he turns to lock my door.

I walk through it quickly, and walk brusquely to the powder room to splash my eyes with cold water. I don't want to go to breakfast looking like this!

I run back out to the hallway where Lorenzo waited for me and I feel ashamed.

"You can come into my room any time you want to," I smile at him broadly and he swoops me up for one last, quick kiss before we start the journey to the dining room.

He takes my breath away and I spend the rest of the walk trying to get it back.

We arrive at the dining room obviously very late. Patrizio looks slightly annoyed, but doesn't let it color his greeting.

"Good morning, my dear! And you Lorenzo," he bows slightly to us both. "What is this look on your face this morning, old friend?" Patrizio circles us looking closely at our faces and wags his finger in the air.

"Ah! What is this? Have we a new dynamic here?" he laughs jovially, with a genuine air of joy.

Lorenzo blushes and looks down at his shoes. I feel mostly like the Morrígan this morning, so I hold my head high and proud, I don't feel like cowering or giving up any of my secrets to Patrizio today. They're mine to keep and I guard them stubbornly.

I think he senses I won't be playing along with his little game, so he gets right to business.

"Miss Walker, I trust you are feeling well this morning, although somewhat late, I'm glad you were able to come to breakfast. I'll need to see you for short meeting after breakfast to brief you on traditions and customs regarding meeting the Pope, and we'll discuss manner of dress and decorum for your meeting with him this afternoon. I need to move on to some other preparations, I'm afraid, so it will just be you and Lorenzo for breakfast this morning, although I get the feeling you don't mind," he winks at me playfully, which despite all my stubborn reserve, does manage to pull a tiny smile out of me - mostly for Lorenzo's benefit. "I'll come back to gather you for the brief when you finish eating. Just send word with one of the wait staff."

"I will, thank you Patrizio."

I am pleasantly surprised that I get to be alone with Lorenzo for breakfast and I walk to the table where he pulls my chair out for me once again, getting me settled in before taking the seat next to me this time.

We start the meal in silence. I feel awkward and unsure about what to say to him, and the silence tells me he must feel the same way, but after a few moments he speaks first.

"I've been in love with you for about a year now . . ."

That's one way to break an awkward silence.

There's a clinking sound as my fork drops to my plate and I nearly choke on the bite I'm in the middle of swallowing. I can feel my eyes bugging and I know I must look completely ridiculous. I swallow hard.

He quickly tries to ease the shock of his revelation. "I still can't say a lot about it before you speak with the

Pope. I'm not authorized to, but I promise you again that you'll understand so much more by this evening and then I'll tell you everything!"

He laughs again. "I knew that you would react in this exact way when I told you. You'd think I could have been a little better prepared to deal with it." He turns back to his plate and stares into it, pushing his food around again.

That's what he was thinking about last night during dinner! He's doing the same thing with his food that he was then. Well this has never happened to me before. What is he thinking? How could he have been in love with me for so long? I didn't even know of him until just before the holidays when I made my trip to New York!

I can see that he's made himself miserable with worry, so I put my hand on his and wrap my fingers around tucking the tips of them into his palm and he squeezes. I can't find my voice, so it's the only thing I can think of to do.

We finish our breakfast without saying anything else. I never think of one thing to say that isn't a question he says he can't answer, so I just continue on in silence hoping he understands.

When the last of the food is gone from our plates, a server clears the table.

"Could you please let Patrizio know we've finished?" I ask him.

"Yes, Miss Walker. I'll let him know."

As Lorenzo and I stand and push in our chairs Patrizio breezes back into the room to round us up for my briefing, leading us to a smallish sitting room only a few hallways and turns later, with a set of french doors that can be closed.

"Please, do sit, Miss Walker," he turns pulling the

doors on tracks out of the wall and closing them.

I sit on a plush, inviting, olive green couch and Lorenzo moves to stand behind me, placing his hands on my shoulders, not hiding our new relationship.

When Patrizio turns and sees us, his eyebrows raise and, his ever-present smile widens and my cheeks flush hot.

"I see I am not wrong about the two of you!" he laughs. "It is of no concern, just please do remember that you are in the Pope's home and treat it respectfully. Do not flaunt any sexual behavior out in the open for others to see. Be sure you keep it behind closed doors."

My cheeks flush an even brighter red, and I am engulfed in a flash of heat that runs the entire length of my body.

Lorenzo is clearly offended. "Sir, I would never do any such thing that might offend his Holiness!"

"Patrizio, if you don't mind, I prefer not to speak of anything even remotely like my private life with you. Can we please agree not to bring anything up again that pertains to the relationship between Lorenzo and myself?"

Well when I least expect it my voice is strong, stern and reasonable.

He is visibly shaken.

"Yes, Miss Walker, I beg your pardon. I forget that American women are so much more conservative than their European counterparts.

Now if you don't mind, I will move on to the business at hand."

I nod and Lorenzo squeezes my shoulders in approval.

"As you know, today you are scheduled to meet the Pope. I understand you are not of the Catholic faith, so what you may not know is what an extreme honor it is to have been invited here."

"I'm not sure you can call it an invitation if I'm not given the option of declining . . . " I mumble.

"I do apologize for the circumstances under which you came to be with us, Miss Walker, but the consensus was that you would never have agreed to come here and this meeting is absolutely vital. What you will learn today is privileged information that very few people in this world or any other, for that matter, can share with you. And if you continue on without it the resulting outcome would, without a doubt, be catastrophic."

Wait, Patrizio and the Catholic Church know that this is not the only world in existence?

My interest is piqued.

"So to get back to the matter at hand, Miss Walker, it is imperative that you dress appropriately for your appointment. I see that you found the new clothes we put in your room. I hope you noticed the variety of clothing, particularly the business clothing. You will need to wear something from that category today and generally look your best.

Now, as for how this will go, you will be taken into a room and will await the Holy Father's entrance at which point you will stand and clap your hands. When he greets you he will extend his hand, but because you are not Catholic you'll not be expected to kiss his ring. You'll shake his hand, instead.

Also, be sure you only address him as 'Your Holiness' or 'Holy Father' and keep any answers to his questions short and to the point. There's no need to ramble on. You'll be permitted to ask him questions as well, but again, keep them succinct.

When he leaves, you'll be expected to remain standing and to watch him leave the room.

Is this all clear, Miss Walker? Do you have any questions for me?"

". . . It sounds easy enough, but . . . really? Stand and clap?"

"Yes, it is the proper thing to do. Please be sure you follow these protocols, otherwise it will appear to him that I have not done my job and I wish to keep my job here at the Vatican, Miss Walker."

"Will I be alone during my meeting or will Lorenzo be going with me?"

"I'm sorry, but Lorenzo won't be with you."

"Okay, well I feel prepared," I tell him. "I promise to remember everything you've told me."

"Thank you, my dear. I will certainly be most grateful if you do. Now, I must be off. I need to see to it that the room for your meeting is prepared." He turns to Lorenzo.

"Miss Walker needs to be outside the ante-room no later than 3:15 this afternoon. Please be sure she is on time, unlike breakfast this morning," he smiles and winks, obviously thinking we were held up for some other reason than why we really were.

He thinks we were having sex! The thought is much less off-putting than I would have expected. *Dammit!* I'm blushing again.

"I'll see you at 3:15 promptly, Miss Walker." He bows and exits the room.

I'm left sitting there in silence with my thoughts churning through images of intimacy with Lorenzo, uncertainty about this afternoon's meeting with the most important religious figure living in the world today, and worrying about whether I'll be able to behave as properly as expected.

Lorenzo walks around the couch and sits down facing me.

"Are you alright?"

I look at his face and I'm struck by how many questions I have for the man in front of me and how utterly pointless it would be for me to ask them yet. The feeling of having to hold them in has me tense and on edge.

"I think I'm fine, I just have a lot on my mind," I tell him.

"I know. I'm sorry. Much of that is my fault. I really shouldn't have dropped that bombshell on you at breakfast. You aren't ready to know about all of that yet. I've just been holding it in for so long. I couldn't do it anymore."

He takes my hands in his and kisses the top of each one, melting any remaining ice hiding in the tiny crevasses of my mind.

Oh boy, I'm in big trouble.

He stands up and pulls me to my feet.

"Let's get you back to your room so you can prepare for this afternoon," he smiles.

On the walk back I'm a giant bundle of nerves. I'm slightly nervous around this man that says he's loved me for a significant amount of time and I'm extremely nervous at the prospect of meeting the Pope today, but I know I have to get things under control.

Lorenzo unlocks my door and lets me inside and I stand in the doorway facing him in the hall. He kisses my cheek and reminds me to be ready to leave my room at 2:50 and I nod.

He starts to close the door, but I put my hand out and hold it open.

"Will you come in and stay with me until it's time for me to go?" I ask him nervously, and he smiles looking nervous too.

"Of course," he says. "Are you sure you want me in your room while you prepare for this afternoon? I know how you like your privacy while you freshen up." He grins teasingly, taking off his blazer, revealing an ill-fitting button up shirt underneath. His muscles bulge, showing through the shape of it.

I tear my eyes away from his physique, forcing myself to put away the thoughts of seeing him without a shirt on.

"Yes, well, yesterday we made friends when you finally told me your name and today you tell me you're in love with me!" I tease back. "How can I kick a guy out who skips from being my kidnapper to my friend to loving me all in one day? I mean, tomorrow we'll be married and starting a family. I'd better get used to you being around!"

He looks abashed.

"Lorenzo, I'm only giving you a hard time!"

He chuckles and tosses his coat in my face, making me laugh.

"Now, how about you come help me choose something to wear. I can't say that I've ever put on a suit before. I have no idea what goes with what and I noticed on the plane that you're quite good at dressing yourself. Maybe you could help dress me?"

He laughs again and takes my hand, once again leading me to the armoire in my bedroom. He opens the doors, stands me in front of it, and moves to stand behind me. He pushes my hair aside and whispers very close to my ear.

"Now pick the pair of slacks you like best, or your favorite color and I'll help you build something around that." At the end of the sentence he plants a soft kiss on my neck, then pulls away.

Oh, he isn't going to make it easy for me to be good, is he? My skin tingles and I break out in goose pimples from head to toe.

I browse through my new clothes and find a pair of light grey slacks that look nice. I pull them off their hanger and hand them to Lorenzo. He smiles.

"Grey. Nice choice . . . *and* an easy choice to build around."

I step out of the way and he sifts through the clothes pulling out, one by one: a matching grey, long suit coat, a black belt, a heather colored, button-down-collar shirt and a pair of black pumps after hovering over, then passing up a pair of black dress shoes with a higher heel.

I lean in and pick them up. "Why not these?"

He looks at me doubtfully. "Can you walk in shoes like that?"

"Humph! Good point." I chuckle. *He really does seem to know me. He knows that I like purple and can't wear super high heels. What else does he know?*

I take the clothes from him and lay them neatly on the bed, then walk back to the armoire and pull out a silky robe I spotted last night, along with a pair of clean panties and bra.

"I'll be back in a few minutes," I say. "Make yourself comfortable . . . *in* my room, not outside the door." I wink.

He smiles and follows me out of the bedroom passing

by the bathroom door to head into the sitting room. I get in the bath, get clean, get out, get toweled off, get my under garments on, and slip into my robe. I brush my teeth again (*one can never brush one's teeth too much*), dry my hair, and brush it out smooth.

I emerge from the bathroom feeling refreshed and squeaky-clean, to see Lorenzo on the couch in the sitting room with his nose in the copy of Alice in Wonderland I was reading yesterday. I giggle and turn the opposite way into the bedroom to get dressed.

I carefully put on the pants and the shirt, tuck it in, thread the belt through the loops on my pants and buckle it. I twirl the coat around my shoulders, slipping first my left arm then my right into their respective sleeves, straighten everything out, put my shoes on, and take a peek in the mirror.

I don't even look like me!

I carefully walk to the door of the sitting room, getting used to the pumps.

"Psst!"

Lorenzo looks up from the book, startled.

"Wow! You look incredible!" he says smiling from ear to ear.

"Well, there's this great guy I know who helped me pick out my clothes . . . " I giggle.

He laughs and checks his watch. "Well we have a little while still. It's about noon."

I roll my eyes. "Ugh! What am I going to do until it's time for my meeting?"

"I'm a little beat. Jet lag," he says. "Feel like a short nap?"

"Ha. I'm always up for a nap . . . " I turn and walk back to the bedroom and he follows me. I cut my eyes at him and start stripping out of my clothes piece by piece, and lay them out neatly on the bench at the foot of my bed, curious to see what his reaction will be.

Lorenzo stops in his tracks, eyes wide.

"What? You don't expect me to lay down in these clothes and get them all wrinkled? They've obviously been pressed and I want to look nice!"

"I . . . I just . . ." he stammers and it's my turn to laugh at him.

"You don't think I actually believe you've never seen me in my underwear!"

He blushes and looks down at his shoes like an embarrassed child.

"Lorenzo, you said I would understand by tonight, so I'm trusting you. If you've seen me sleep, chances are you've seen me nude at times."

He doesn't look up, so I put the robe on, cross the room to where he stands, and look up at him, smiling.

"It's okay. I'm not mad. Besides, I can't pass any judgement until I know the full extent of everything. I don't understand anything at this point," I stand on my tip-toes craning my neck to kiss him. He takes one look at me and pounces, kissing me passionately, picking me up and carrying me to the bed. He sets me down and falls to the bed with me.

My body is responding to him involuntarily, while my mind is telling me to slow down. *He's obviously been holding this back for a long time, but I've only had a couple of days with him. It's too soon for me.*

I break away. "Lorenzo, forgive me. I'm not ready for this. I didn't mean to make you think otherwise. I shouldn't have gotten undressed in front of you. I made a mistake."

His smile is kind and understanding. He lightly kisses my forehead, my eyebrows, my nose, each cheek, then barely kisses my mouth.

"Dana, you don't need to apologize to me. This can go at any pace you want it to. I have been waiting for you for quite a while now. I can wait as long as you need me to."

I snuggle into his chest and he wraps his arms around me, making me feel so at home that I relax immediately. It's both confusing and comforting at the same time, but I just trust that I'll know what to make of it soon enough.

After a peaceful sleep my eyes flutter open and I check Lorenzo's watch.

1:45. No need to get up just yet.

I watch my bedfellow sleep, studying how his features change when they're completely relaxed and listening to him breathe. I feel so strange with him, like I've known him forever. Normally I would probably be completely freaked out by this, but after my experience with Bébinn, nothing seems weird anymore.

Where is Bébinn? I would have thought she would be here by now.

"I'm here, Sister. I'm in Rome. I've just been listening, trying to get some idea of what's going on."

"Oh! Have you now?" I smile to myself, *"You are a snake!"*

"Well, when I got here it was obvious that your stress level was low and then there's the matter of this Lorenzo person. Who is he?"

"It's a long story and I actually don't even know it all yet, but he's the man from New York that chased me down and we saw him in Fourknocks. Remember?"

"Wait, from what I've been hearing you think, it seems like there are some new feelings for him or something? What about Séamus? Have you forgotten that he hurt Séamus? And he's been trying to

kill you!"

"Man you sound a lot like the voice of reason that I banished yesterday . . . I know it seems crazy, but there's more to this, I feel it, know it. He says there's a lot he can't tell me because he isn't authorized to and I'll know it all after I talk to the Pope today. Not only that, the Morrígan knows him."

After a long pause.

"Are you there?"

"Yes . . . just thinking. I hadn't heard that part."

"I still can't hear you do that!"

Bébinn laughs.

"Hmm, the Morrígan knows him? Well this is an interesting development. I'll wait to hear more from your meeting today, but . . . if this is true . . . well, I'll just wait. You should find it all out on your own."

"Gee . . . thanks."

"What? You should be used to this by now."

I check Lorenzo's watch again and it's 2:30.

"Éire, it's time for me to get ready for my meeting. I'll check in with you tonight? Do you have a place to stay?"

"Yes, don't worry about me, just concentrate on what's happening there."

"Okay, I'll talk with you soon. Hopefully I'll get to see you soon!"

"Lorenzo," I soften my voice and kiss him on the cheek. *It's a shame to have to wake him up. Now I know what he meant this morning.*

He stirs and opens his eyes, looking up into mine. A giant smile breaks out on his face and he closes his eyes again.

"Am I dreaming?"

I laugh softly. "No, but it's time to get up now. I need to get redressed and you need to go to the sitting room."

His eyes are still closed and he's still smiling.

"I've waited so long to wake and see you above me."

I gently lean down and touch my lips to his while his eyes are still closed and he wraps his arms around me again. We kiss like this for a few minutes and I know if I don't get up and get going we will be late.

That can't happen.

I jump off the bed and grab his hands pulling with all my might. I'm surprised that I'm able to pull him up to a sitting position, but I'm sure I didn't do it by myself.

We laugh together.

"I just want to stay here with you all day, no interruptions," he says.

"Yes, and *I* just want to find out everything there is to know about this insane situation I'm in."

He looks dejected. "I know," then his face brightens, "but tonight will be a good night!"

"Ok, I believe you," I laugh and he checks his watch and jumps off the bed, running to the sitting room.

"Dana, what are you doing? You've got to get dressed! Hurry up!"

Oh boy, I really am in trouble. I shake my head, picking up my pants and stepping into them.

I dress quickly, but carefully, check everything in the mirror and all looks to be in place. I walk out to the sitting room.

"Everything still okay?" I ask gesturing to my outfit, and Lorenzo looks at me, stands and strides over, taking my face in his hands and kisses me again, passionately, a little roughly and for a half second I want to take him back in my bedroom and get back into bed.

"You look incredible, Dana. You should feel great going into this meeting. You look fantastic; you're a very smart woman. Just be yourself and you'll do wonderfully."

I exhale a puff of breath I must have been holding. *Gotta remember to breathe.*

He checks his watch again and it must be time to go. He picks up his jacket and puts it on, then leads me to the door, unlocks it, pulls me through, then locks it again. We make the trip to the ante-room without touching or talking. I'm just too distracted by what I'm about to do.

We arrive outside the door to the ante-room at 3:00 and my palms are sweating.

I don't know why I'm so nervous. It's not like I'm Catholic.

Patrizio walks up almost as soon as we get there.

"Ah, you're on time!" he says in his totally energetic, always happy way. "And Miss Walker! You look absolutely stunning! Thank you for taking that part of this meeting seriously," he bows in my direction and I feel my cheeks get hot again.

Why is it this guy is always making me blush?

"Since you're already here, we'll go ahead and get you settled in. Come with me."

I grab Lorenzo's hand and drag him with me. I want him there as long as he can be before the Pope arrives. Patrizio leads me into the room and I am struck by its grandeur.

The ceiling is tiered and highly decorated. The top of the wall drips with an architectural gold garland, in fact, nearly all decoration in the room is gilded. False square columns extend slightly from the wall, also dripping with decoration, topped with gilded Corinthian capitals. The walls are lined with paintings and mirrors encased in chunky, elaborate gold frames, and in the center of the room hangs a chandelier the size of a small car made of crystal pieces. It reminds me of water spray in a fountain.

My host takes me to a couch upholstered in gold fabric that faces the door and is situated across from a matching couch.

"Please sit here, Miss Walker. And *do* remember what we talked about earlier."

"I will, Patrizio, I promise."

"Okay, then Lorenzo and I will leave you now. You're going to do wonderfully. I am confident."

"Thank you," I say and then look at Lorenzo with a look that I hope says: "help me!" He smiles and shrugs and follows Patrizio back out of the room.

"You'll do fine," he mouths just before walking through the door.

It closes behind him and I am alone in a small gold universe, waiting for a man who is larger than life to come and tell me the gods only know what.

There's a clock on the mantle directly to my right and it ticks loudly, reminding me that I'm waiting, making the five minutes I wait seem like an hour.

The door opens and an elderly man dressed in white walks in alone. I stand and clap my hands as I've been instructed and the butterflies in my stomach are flying wildly in anticipation.

The Pope approaches me smiling and extends his hand. I take it and shake it calmly and he speaks to me in a calming, easy way.

"It's a pleasure to meet you, Miss Walker. Thank you very much for accepting my invitation to visit. I expect your stay is satisfactory?"

"Yes, Your Holiness. The accommodations are absolutely beautiful and I've been provided with everything I need, thank you." *Wonder if he doesn't know that I wasn't given a choice whether to come here or not . . . ?*

"Very good! I'm pleased to hear you say that!" he smiles and gestures to the couch behind me. "Please make yourself comfortable. This conversation is probably going to take some time. There is much we need to discuss."

I sit as gracefully as I can, he does the same and I look at him expectantly.

"First, a formality, I'm afraid. I need to confirm that you are who we've been told you are. Have you the Morrígan's Key in your possession, dear?"

"Yes, Your Holiness," I nod.

"May I see it?" He extends his hand as if asking me to give it to him. So I pull the cord out of my shirt and unhook it, sliding the key off, and holding it in my hand.

"Holy Father, I feel I must warn you that setting the key in your hand will have some undesirable effects. I'm told the shock is unpleasant and it tends to fly off in any direction. I fear for the beautiful decorations in the room if I give it to you this way. May I set it here on this table instead?" I stand and take it to a small side table within his reach.

"Oh! Yes, yes. I should have thought of that myself. Thank you for your concern. Please show me in any way you feel appropriate."

I set the key down and he leans into it like a child might hunker down to get a close look at a particularly interesting bug. He looks at it approvingly, but doesn't reach for it as most people do, only studies it.

"May I pick it up? I know that the Prophecy says I won't be able to, but I would like to try with your permission."

177

"Of course, Your Holiness."

He extends his hand slowly and the key just as slowly moves away, as it always does. Part of me wondered if he might be different and might be able to pick it up, only because of who he is. He watches it move across the table a couple inches more, then looks up at me and smiles.

"I'm satisfied, Miss Walker. I knew who you were as soon as you produced the key, I just wanted to see if the stories were true!" he laughs heartily and it makes me laugh, putting me at ease with him.

He's a fun person, has a sense of humor. That's comforting.

I quickly put the key back on its cord and tuck it back into my shirt.

The Pope's face darkens and takes on a serious expression.

"In the past months I know that you have been aware of a perceived danger, actually, let me step back a little bit and say that the Catholic Church has changed over the hundreds of years of its existence. We are aware that there are other gods and goddesses and we're also aware of the many, many worlds that exist besides our own. We know of the Prophecy and take it seriously. We also acknowledge that in the past our closed-mindedness and refusal to allow other religions and practices to flourish has changed our world significantly for the worse. It has created a global society of intolerance and ignorance that is now coming to light for us. I am determined to allow the Prophecy to play itself out.

But as you know, Popes of the past have been much more rigid in their insistence that the Catholic Church is the only true Church and that our God is the only god there is.

The Knights Templar formed themselves together as defenders of Christianity, and then upon adoption by the Church on Papal authority, they were repurposed secretly and solely for the mission to destroy the Morrígan, who it was said was tasked by the Earth Mother with protecting her from the far reaches of the Catholic Church. Back then, the Church viewed every other religion and lifestyle as a threat to her very existence and vowed to wipe them all from the lands they had under their control at that time. Thus the Druids, who were the chosen people of the Goddess Brighid to take care of the Earth Mother and protect our planet from the destructive tendencies of Human Beings, were all but wiped out by the Church.

The Church of the Dark Ages found a way to send Templars through time and one of them discovered that the Morrígan had been reborn as a young woman in the New World." He pauses.

"Lorenzo?" I ask.

"Absolutely not, Miss Walker! Lorenzo works for me.

When it became apparent to us that the Templar knew who you were, we realized you needed round the clock protection. Those men were to be taken seriously.

So I hope you'll forgive us for the intrusion into your life. Lorenzo has been watching you mostly from afar, but lately the Templar has gotten more bold and come much closer to you than in the past. I suspect it is because of your increased power and awareness of the Morrígan's presence. We knew it was only a matter of time.

Incidentally, upon my coronation, when my tolerance for other religions and views came to light, it became necessary to increase my security as well. The Church of the past is not at all happy with the Church of the present, namely me."

He waves his hand as if to brush aside his thoughts.

"But I digress. I did bring you here to give you some history on this, but I also asked you here to give you another message from Merlin."

My jaw drops open and I close it again as fast as I can, remembering my manners.

"How can you possibly know Merlin? Have you been to the Otherworld as well?"

"No, Merlin has come to me. News of my changed views of the Church spread far and wide fairly quickly and he thought we could help ensure your survival so that you're able to bring the Prophecy to fruition.

Merlin's message is simple: The Morrígan's key opens the Morrígan's door."

I stare at him blankly. *That's a message? It doesn't even say anything!*

He sees that I'm bewildered. "I know, I'm sorry. It is somewhat ambiguous, but Merlin assures me that when it's time to use the key, you'll know, without a doubt, what this message means."

I nod to him concededly. "Yes, Your Holiness, I'm sure that is correct. Nothing is ever as it seems anymore, so when I am truly confused about something, I trust that what is unknown to me will soon reveal itself somehow."

"How right you are, young Sage. You are absolutely worthy of your title - wise beyond your years."

"Thank you, Holy Father." I smile, pleased that he approves of me.

"There is nothing else I am able to tell you, young lady. That was all I have been entrusted with. Again accept my gratitude that you chose to come and hear my message." He extends his hand and I take it, preparing to shake it once again, but he makes the sign of the cross and says a blessing over me, which as a pleasant surprise, feels very similar to one of Aurelia's kisses.

"Thank you, Holy Father!"

"You're very welcome, Miss Walker. I wish you much luck and bid you a good day." With that he turns and strides out of the room and I keep my eyes on him as he exits, just as Patrizio instructed.

As the door closes, I collapse on the couch and breathe a great sigh of relief.

"Bébinn, did you hear?"

"Yes, I heard everything that you thought anyway, you may need to fill me in on some of the details."

"Lorenzo is not the Templar! He was hired by the Catholic Church to watch over me and protect me from the Templar who's been hunting me down."

"That's wonderful news! Thank goodness you haven't fallen in love with a crazy person! I was worried, but it makes much more sense now that the Morrígan knows him."

"Fallen in love? I . . . don't know . . . maybe? What can you tell me about his connection to the Morrígan?"

"Nothing just yet. I still think you need to talk to him and find out on your own."

"You're exasperating, Sister!"

"I may be, but I'm right. You'll see . . . " she laughs.

The door to the room opens and Patrizio strolls in with Lorenzo on his heels.

"Éire, I'll talk to you more a little later."

The two men are beaming at me. "Young lady, I am told that you did exceptionally well in your meeting!" Patrizio calls to me, arms outstretched. He hugs me and kisses me on each cheek. I laugh at his excitement.

"Well, I'm so glad you approve, Mr. Borghi." I act out a playful curtsey, despite the fact that I'm not wearing a dress.

I turn my attention to Lorenzo, and his pride is written all over his face.

"You must have been perfect," he says quietly, taking me in his arms. He kisses me and again I feel myself melt and the room falls away, spinning out from under me. Soon I am floating in this world of Dana and Lorenzo.

The sound of Patrizio clearing his throat brings us crashing back to reality, planting our feet firmly back on the floor.

We break our embrace and look at him, embarrassed.

"Ah young love," he laughs, clasping his hands together under his chin. "You'll be excused from the evening meal tonight so the two of you can go out and celebrate on your own, if you'd like."

"Actually, along those lines," Lorenzo begins. "Patrizio, would you mind taking Dana back to her room for me? There's something I need to take care of this afternoon." He looks at me. "I'll be back this evening around 6:00, okay?"

I smile. "Okay, sure. I'll see you then."

We all walk through the door and Lorenzo turns to the right, Patrizio and I turn to the left and walk back in the direction of my rooms.

"I'm very proud of you, Miss Walker. I will say I was slightly worried. You've got quite the stubborn streak and I thought you might just throw protocol to the wind."

I only laugh.

"You know . . . Lorenzo has been quite taken with you for a very long time. His devotion to you has long since moved past that required by his job. You won't find a more loyal friend." I smile at him, not sure what to say to that. It's still so new to me.

We walk in silence for a couple of turns.

"Oh! Did you know that he is also a Druid?"

I turn to him in shock! "No! He hasn't said one word about it or showed me anything that might indicate that he is."

"Lorenzo is a very modest man. He doesn't like to draw attention to himself at all. He was the reason your friend Séamus survived the Templar's attack. He followed your crows realizing they were letting him know something was horribly wrong and he arrived at Séaums's house just in time. He fought off the Templar and placed a protective spell on your friend. He should have died from his wounds, but Lorenzo's spell sustained his life until you were able to close the wounds and heal him."

I am speechless. Our lives are much more intertwined than I could have ever imagined. *My crows? Never thought of them as mine. How did he know to follow them?*

"Wow," is all I manage to get out.

Patrizio laughs at me. "I know this is all a lot to process, but you've been processing new ideas and strange happenings for months now. Aren't you getting used to it at all, yet?"

"Not really," I reply. "I should be, but to a regular, unremarkable girl this stuff is completely off the wall and out of left field. It's beyond my wildest imagination!"

"Oh, but Miss Walker, you're anything but unremarkable!"

"I never knew anything about that until October! Until then I had never done anything even slightly out of the ordinary. Then all in one afternoon I find out I can draw and sing things into being, and I've suddenly got this faerie companion? You have to admit it would be hard to come to terms with."

"I suppose I could understand that," he smiles and gestures that we've arrived at my door. He opens it and lets me go through, locking it behind me, bidding me a good night.

"I'll see you tomorrow, Miss Walker."

"Yes, until tomorrow, Mr. Borghi."

CHAPTER ELEVEN

The Morrigan's Door

I walk straight to the armoire. *Time to get back into something more comfortable, then relax for a while.*

I hang up my slacks, coat, and shirt; put away my shoes and belt, then put on the most comfortable pair of jeans I can find. I pull a t-shirt over my head and root through the hoodies hanging there until I find one that feels particularly soft and cozy. I put my arms through the sleeves and zip it up.

Then I walk back to the sitting room where I plan to sit down with my copy of Alice in Wonderland and read until Lorenzo gets back.

Only moments after I sit down, though, I hear a scratching noise at the window.

What in the world?

The noise stops and I push it out of my thoughts, diving back into my book. I read only a few more pages before I hear it again.

Okay, what is going on?

I flop the book down, spine up, open to the place I left off, and stand up to go see what's going on. When I pull back the curtains there are three crows standing on the sill outside the window, pecking and scratching at the glass.

There are crows outside my window . . . trying to get in?

Bébinn interjects. *"Morrígan, you need to keep alert and be aware of your surroundings. Those crows are not a good sign. I'm coming to find you right now."*

"Okay, but how are you going to get in here?"

"Don't worry, I'll find a way. Lorenzo is with you, isn't he?"

"No, he's away for the afternoon. He said there was something he needed to do."

"There's someone outside your door, right?! Tell me they didn't leave you unguarded!"

"I'm not sure, I think so, but . . . Patrizio was the only one around when I came back to my room and I doubt he stayed to keep watch."

"I'll be there as quickly as I can, Morrígan. Don't let anyone in your room unless you're absolutely positive it's Lorenzo, okay?"

"Okay."

I'm a little nervous, but I feel pretty safe here in the Papal apartments.

It would be next to impossible for someone to get in here that wasn't invited. Especially since as the Pope said to me earlier, they've increased Papal security.

I close the curtains again, blocking out the crows and return to the couch, where I pick up my book and continue reading. From time to time I hear the scratching at the glass and try to think of it as company instead of a bad sign, but the sounds steadily increase in intensity as it gets darker.

I put the book down again after about an hour and four chapters of reading and go back to the window. There are at least twenty crows scratching and vying for a place on the window sill now, and beyond the window hundreds of them perch on the surrounding roofs.

I drop the curtain.

"Éire, there are hundreds of crows . . . "

I wait . . .

No response.

I hear the key in the lock. *Lorenzo's back!* I'm so relieved.

Taking a few steps toward the door, I remember Éire's warning: "Don't let anyone in unless you're sure it's Lorenzo".

"Lorenzo?"

The doorknob stops moving and there's silence on the other side. "Bébinn?!" I call out, fear heavy in my stomach like a large ball of lead. Stepping backward, away from the door realizing that something is very, very wrong, I look back to the window again where it sounds as if the crows are now throwing themselves against the glass.

There's a loud thud against the door and I whip my head around just in time to see it splinter at the latch and swing open wildly. The Templar stands in the doorway wielding a mace and a shield, looking at me as if sizing me up momentarily before rushing into the room. I scream at the top of my lungs, hoping someone will hear and sometime between running for the bedroom door, screaming, and being chased by the Templar, Lorenzo bursts into the room.

He rushes the Templar from behind, swinging a bottle of wine in a wide arc, smashing it into the face opening of the Templar's helmet, blinding him.

"Run, Dana! Run and don't look back. We're not sure how many of these guys there are!"

The Templar struggles against Lorenzo's restraint, scratching at his face with his free hand to try to clear the glass and wine away. I am paralyzed with fear, standing still, staring in amazement.

"GO!" Lorenzo bellows at me in anger and it's just what I need to get my feet moving. I run out of the door and down the hall, passing a bunch of flowers on the floor not far from my room.

I run as fast as my feet can carry me, trying desperately to remember all the turns we take to the dining hall, which I think is close to the entrance. Against all odds I finally make it there and I can see the entrance through a doorway.

Thank the Gods I was right!

I stop long enough to take a couple of breaths before rushing to the front door. I throw it open and burst through, further confusing the fellows in the crazy colored uniforms who seem to be pretty confused already, pointing at the birds and chattering to each other in Italian.

With renewed vigor my feet again find their forward momentum when I hear a clamber behind me. The Templar has somehow gained the upper hand, in spite of his bleeding face, and is on my trail again.

Lorenzo! Bébinn, you've got to help me! Where are you? I need you!

"I'm coming, Sister! I'm sorry, there's more than one Templar. I've just dealt with a small band of them. I'm on my way!"

Tears of worry for Lorenzo are streaming down my face, but he would be so angry with me if I didn't save myself.

I run straight through the murder of crows stirring them up and they scatter like fall leaves. I glance behind me and see that it doesn't take long for them to regroup and swarm the Templar, but he doesn't seem very bothered by it. He keeps running after me, extending his left arm like a visor in front of his head to keep them from getting at his already mangled face.

Darkness has descended on Rome. My footfalls . . . on the cobblestone streets . . . the sound is echoing off the strange buildings surrounding me, mixing with the cawing of the crows. I can hear the Templar's feet pounding as well.

My blood runs ice cold. *My dream.*

"Bébinn, my dream! I'm living my dream. This is it!"

"Hold on, Morrígan, I'm on my way! I swear I'll be there soon!"

I push myself to just keep running and running, my legs and lungs burning and side splitting, but if I stop . . .

I can't think about it. I just have to go.

The crows behind me are deafening, their screaming ringing in my ears. I imagine them pecking at the Templar with satisfaction.

There's a side street up ahead and I duck down it, desperate for refuge, some place to hide, but when I see where I am, the cold hand of fear grips me and roots me to the spot. I'm staring down the street I ran down in my dream. My heart is racing from exertion and fear and I know: This is the end of my life. I saw it here in this very place.

My world stands still, all sound falls away, I see my parents wave goodbye to me at the airport, I see Aurelia flying through the field like a crazy faerie after I fixed her wings, then I see Séamus's face and his voice comes to me:

"Visions are not prophetic. Nothin' is set in stone . . . "

Change the future!

A gust of wind pushes against my back. The crows burst onto the street, pushing me forward, and I start running again just in time. The Templar is right behind me, but the crows are still working on him. I run and run and the church from my dream comes into view ahead.

Change the future!

But there's nowhere else to go. I'm panicked, frantically looking for something to do other than run into that church, but there's nothing. I have no choice. I take the steps three at a time, pushing open it's heavy door, but the time it takes for me to get the door open is exactly what the Templar needs to make up the distance between us.

"You!" He screams at me in English, grabbing me by the hair, pushing me further into the church, down the aisle to the altar. "What a fitting place for me to put you to death!"

He slings me roughly around to face him, then picks me up and throws me as hard as he can onto my back on the stone floor of the altar. I black out for an instant as my head hits the floor, but I force myself to regain consciousness.

I have to fight!

"Bébinn!" I scream out!

"I'm here!" she says from somewhere outside the church.

"Wait!" Lorenzo's voice . . .

But before I can move, the Templar un-sheaths his knife and plunges it into my chest just as I saw him do in the dream.

"It's too late, Bébinn . . ."

The metallic smell of blood and the burning sensation

in my chest overwhelms me. I put my hand to my chest and feel that it's wet. It slips around over my heart and I can't make it stay still. *Need to stop the bleeding. I can stop. Lorenzo, where are you? Bébinn? Stop the blood.*

My thoughts are getting jumbled.

The Templar disappears from my view and Lorenzo's crying face, distorted with sorrow, looms over me, just as I saw him in the dream.

He looks away from me, yelling out. "Hurry! You've got to hurry. She needs us *now*!"

He is mumbling something I can't understand through his sobs.

"Mi dispiace, il mio amore, mi dispiace, mi . . . dispiace."

My chest burns like it's on fire, but cold is spreading through the rest of my body. My eyelids are heavy.

I'll just take a short nap and then I'll get up and go find help . . .

"No Morrígan! Don't leave me! Stay with me, don't close your eyes!"

But I can't keep them open.

"Éire, I can't . . . I can't stay . . . open. My chest . . . hurts. Tired."

Then . . . there is no floor beneath me, no roof above me, no sky overhead, only infinity.

A flash of light, a door, an image of me drawing the lock, music then the door is real, a shift in consciousness . . .

The pain is gone and there's something on my face and my chest. I open my eyes and Lorenzo is covering my face with kisses, his tears wetting my cheeks. I feel so tired and disoriented.

I blink quickly, we're surrounded by candlelight and . . . crows?

"What's going on?" I croak, my throat dry and voice hoarse.

Lorenzo sits up covered in blood.

My eyebrows knit in concern. "Lorenzo! Are you okay?"

He looks down at me in surprise, then at Bébinn. She holds her trembling hands to her mouth. They're also covered in blood.

"Dana!" she wails. "I didn't think you were coming back to us!"

"Bébinn! The key . . . !"

I raise my own bloody hands to my throat searching for it and relief washes over me when I feel it on the cord, just where it should be.

"I know what it's for. I know what I'm supposed to do . . . "

I struggle to sit up, but my body is weak.

Lorenzo lifts me to a sitting position and everything that just happened comes flooding back to me!

"Wait, you didn't think I was coming back . . . ? Did I . . . ?"

She looks at me with tears streaming down her face too. I look from her to Lorenzo, then back to my sister.

"I died . . . didn't I?"

Bébinn nods her head slowly. "Lorenzo and I pooled our magic, but I wasn't sure it was going to be enough. Thankfully he's very powerful. Only a fully trained Druid of the Druid Order would have enough power to combine with mine to repair a wound like that. I wish you could have seen it work. It was amazing!"

Lorenzo pulls me into his chest smashing me to him.

"I'm so glad you're here, you're ok! I have no idea how we managed that. I was out of my mind!"

My face breaks out into a smile like I've never felt before. I have a sister, a faerie, lots of new friends, and a . . . Lorenzo.

"Let's go," I say. "I'm going to need a few things before I open the door."

Bébinn looks at me with a questioning look.

"The key. The Morrígan's key opens the Morrígan's door," I say as if it makes all the sense in the world. "I saw everything I need to do while I was . . . gone."

Lorenzo shakes his head at me. "I'm just glad you're walking away from this."

He stands me up and they support me, my sister under my left arm, my Lorenzo under my right. The three of us, looking like we've murdered someone, step over the Templar's body and head out into the street.

"What happened to him?" I jerk my head backward in the direction of the church.

"Oh, we'll tell you the whole thing over a bottle of wine."

CHAPTER TWELVE

Resources

A note from the Author on Rape:

It took me years to admit to anyone that I was ever sexually assaulted in high school. My parents were oblivious, my friends had no idea, and I suffered in a private hell of guilt and shame for years afterward. When I was young the internet was just getting started and we couldn't go to our favorite search engine and get the kind of search results you can today. I felt alone and isolated with nowhere to turn.

Now I know that wasn't the case. Here a few facts you may not know about sexual assault:

In America someone is sexually assaulted every two minutes, and each year there are about 237,878 victims of sexual assault.

44% of those victims are under the age of 18 and 80% are under the age of 30.

* * *

60% of rapes are never reported and 97% of rapists will never spend a day in jail.

Approximately 2/3 of sexual assaults are committed by someone known to the victim and 38% of rapists are a friend or acquaintance of the victim.

If you are a victim of sexual assault please get help.

http://www.rainn.org

CPSIA information can be obtained
at www.ICGtesting.com
Printed in the USA
FSOW01n0023080615
7719FS

9 781630 687427